Last Train to M

At 50 years old Poppy was finally ready to leave her home in London and embark upon a new adventure, the little seaside resort of Margate was calling. Elderly Aunt Flora had offered her a home at rambling Lookout Retreat, and it was time for Poppy to mend all of her broken pieces. When she noticed the small card in the window of the Madam Popoff Vintage Emporium informing the curious public, *"Part time help required. Only special people need apply,"* Poppy is drawn into a world of wonder, magic and true healing. As the clocks ticked on Poppy often asked herself, "Exactly who is Madam Popoff, an old shopkeeper with a wizened face? Gypsy? Fairy Godmother? Angel? Time Traveller? Gate Keeper?"

Reflecting upon her first year's sojourn at the Madam Popoff Vintage Emporium, Poppy looked down at her own long slender fingers and her delicate hands, working with Madam had taught her the importance of her hands. She had learned to feel her way through life, to discern stories and ownership just by touching the things that crossed Madam's threshold. Poppy acknowledged that there's a silver thread that connects people, places, events and time. Now she was also beginning to understand the mysteries of healing. She knew in her heart that being in Margate had set her upon a path of healing herself, but more than this she was learning how she might be of assistance to others in distress.

Poppy had become privy to many stories: an exquisite art deco clutch bag decorated with beaded irises blowing in the wind connected her to the Margate lifeboat and the 1940 evacuation of Dunkirk. A little gold donkey brooch with a seed pearl eye connected her to the trenches, the futility and utter devastation of the First World War. A faded, yet still jaunty, knitted Superman doll connected her to 1972 and a little boy suffering from severe spinal malformation. His adventures with Superman helped him to live vicariously in a world outside the confines of a spinal cast. An old Beatles album connected Poppy to The Royal School for Deaf Children, the 1963 Beatles performance in Margate, and with two deaf friends who were inseparable.

One day a little booklet called *"The Twelve Healers,"* written by Dr. Edward Bach and published in 1933 had crossed Madam's threshold, and Poppy also began to learn about the superior healers of mankind. As she grew in wisdom and knowledge Poppy accepted that, *"In the end three things matter; how much you loved, how gently you lived, and how gracefully you let go of things not meant for you."*

This book is about the passage of time and a lovely little seaside resort but it could be any town, anywhere in the world. It is about life and the ups-and-downs that we all experience. A series of short stories explore sorrow and joy, hardship and loss. There are people who leave behind a legacy of kindness, sacrifice and courage. Other people suffer from the repercussions that overindulgence and selfishness bring. *"Last Train to Margate"* explores the forces of light and darkness and the possibility that Madam Popoff is a Master from beyond this world.

Last Train to Margate

Sally Forrester

BookLocker

Published by BookLocker.com, Inc., St. Petersburg, Florida.

Printed on acid-free paper.

The characters and events in this book are fictitious. Any similarity to real persons, living or dead, is coincidental and not intended by the author.

The author, Sally Forrester, took the front cover photograph, *Another Time* by the British sculptor Sir Antony Gormley, OBE. Sally also took the three photographs shown on the back cover. Winston is in the bicycle basket!

BookLocker.com, Inc.
2019

First Edition

Disclaimer

This book may offer health information, but this information is designed for educational, and entertainment purposes only. The content does not and is not intended to convey medical advice and does not constitute the practice of medicine. You should not rely on this information as a substitute for, nor does it replace, professional medical advice, diagnosis, or treatment. The author and publisher are not responsible for any actions taken based on information within.

Dedication

To the fond memory of my very loving mum and dad, Evelyn and Pat Forrester, to my dear uncle, Len Hewson, and to the brave lifeboat men of *The Lord Southborough* and the Margate Surf Boat, *Friend To All Nations.*

About the Author

Sally's parents, Pat and Evelyn Forrester, came to Margate in the late 1940s on their honeymoon; they loved it so much that they stayed. Sally was born and grew up in the little town, and first left when she finished St. George's School and attended teacher-training college. Although she moved to the USA with her husband and two sons in 1994 Sally always returns, usually for several months during the summertime, and to celebrate Christmas with relatives. Over the years she has witnessed the town decline and rise once again in fortune. Margate is in her blood and holds a special place in her heart. This is Sally's first novel; she has worked as a teacher, artist and in the holistic health field. Her passion is to help people get well and enjoy life. Sally weaves her extensive knowledge and experience of healing with herbs, homoeopathy and flower remedies into the book and draws her inspiration from the many suffering people who, over the years, have come to tell their story.

The upturn in fortunes of old town Margate inspired Sally to set her book in the Madam Popoff Vintage Emporium. Yes, it is a real shop and a delightful place but the Madam Popoff of "Last Train to Margate" is purely a work of fiction, as are the things that cross Madam's threshold, the characters, and their stories. However, Sally does draw upon the colourful history of Margate and the surrounding area, and some of the people and events are factual, this becomes clear as the reader enjoys the book.

Sally met Mary and her little dog, Winston, at Ship Shape Café in Ramsgate and they too are real. Winston loves his daily sausage dished out by the doting café staff. She also draws upon her knowledge of the Margate Lifeboat. Her father, Pat Forrester, was part of the launching crew before his untimely death in 1981. Her mother was a member of Margate Ladies Lifeboat Guild and for many years, before moving to the

USA, Sally was chairman of the Woodley, Berkshire Fundraising Branch of The Royal National Lifeboat Institution.

When Sally is at home in the USA she enjoys sailing her yacht around the coastal waters of Florida and consulting with the many families who seek out her help,

Chapter 1

Poppy glanced up at the clock in St. Pancras Station. Time was moving fast; she had a few minutes to reach her platform and board the last train that day to Margate. At 50 years old she didn't move quite as fast as she did in her younger days but she was still agile and fit. Clutching her roller case in one hand and a large bouquet purchased from Marks and Spencer in the other she made a dash across the station and jumped aboard as the train's whistle blew.

Poppy collapsed in an ungainly heap and checked her watch and quietly muttered to herself, "Yes, 23.12 the last train to Margate!" It was early July and already unbearably hot in London. The papers were full of global warming threats and Poppy felt unsettled. Actually Poppy was unsettled in many ways for she was about to embark upon a new chapter in her life. She had taken a leap into the unknown; her ship had finally left the safety of the harbour and she was risking everything and heading towards Margate.

Margate had come up in the world. Somewhere, a few years back, she had read that it was the eighth most desirable place to live. It was Aunt Flora who had instructed her to come. "Sell up my dear, move to the seaside, and start again." Aunt Flora was wise but she was also just a little bit crazy. Poppy pictured her right now as she slumped back in her train seat and drew in a deep breath. Aunt Flora was distinguished, tall and elegant. Snowy white hair, thick and shiny, adorned her head and on top of it all she liked to wear a modest tiara whenever the occasion permitted!

Flora liked to dance, attending all the tea dances around Margate and beyond. She liked to dress up and drink tea out of elegant gold-rimmed, bone china cups from a bygone age. She lived in a rambling flint house over-looking the sea with her snappy little Chihuahua dog aptly named, Sir Humphrey, and a delightful Jack Russell terrier called Jack the Lad.

Poppy was reflecting for a while upon Aunt Flora's unswerving friendship and support throughout the really tough times in her life, and then suddenly she began to panic. The decision to sell her London flat, gift some of her most treasured possessions, pack up and store other things that she couldn't part with and hand in her notice at the office where she worked as a highly regarded personal assistant were all behind her now. Margate awaited her arrival and it really scared her.

The last train thundered through the night and Poppy smiled, as she smelt the beautiful pink and yellow roses in her bouquet. Aunt Flora would be pleased. She loved beautiful things, the walled garden surrounding her rambling home facing the sea would be full of flowers carefully tended by Flora and Fred her trusty old gardener. Flora and Fred had tamed Lookout Retreat's garden for many years, and it was their pride and joy.

Poppy was anxious because she had never been one to easily make a decision, and it had taken her several years to finally pluck up enough courage to turn her back on the hustle, bustle and bright lights of London to embark upon a new adventure. Then there was tiredness, Poppy was deeply tired, tired to the bone. Energy was lacking, zest for life was gone, dark circles cleverly concealed by makeup told the story. Too much stress, too much disappointment, too many failed relationships, too much anguish and too much fear had taken their toll. Poppy was a wilted rose and with that thought she sighed and fell into a deep sleep.

A sudden jolt broke the silence and Poppy's slumber; the train's intercom announced that they had arrived in Broadstairs. "Gosh!" Exclaimed Poppy, "the next stop is Margate." She rose to her feet, straightened her crumpled dress, gathered up her backpack, handbag, roller case and bouquet and began to head down the carriage towards the doors.

Margate station hadn't changed much since her last visit and Poppy also remembered it from wonderful childhood visits to Aunt Flora and Uncle Bertie. The Victorian station had received a coat of paint but not much else had changed. It was very late, the reception hall was closed and signs guided passengers around the side to the station forecourt where a couple of taxi drivers waited patiently for fares. The air was fresh with a salty tang, stars lit up the inky blackness and there was a faint smell of fish and chips and vinegar.

Chapter 2

Poppy glided quietly through the heavy oak door of Lookout Retreat, Aunt Flora had kindly left the key under a pot of geraniums. She slipped quickly into the starched, crisp cotton sheets of the huge sleigh bed in one of the guest rooms. It was her favourite room overlooking the sea, the one with little blue forget-me-not flowers on the wallpaper. She slept peacefully until the herring gulls began their early morning reeling calls.

Flora, dressed in an elegant silk kimono dressing gown, knocked and entered with a welcoming cup of tea set out on a porcelain tray laid with a lace cloth; this was to be the beginning of endless cups of tea before Poppy finally got her life in order.

Aunt Flora was of course delighted to have a companion to share her home. It was a cavernous place with far too many rooms for one person. When Bertie was alive it had been filled with music, laughter and joy. They would dance in the hallway under the crystal chandeliers. Flora would wear her tiaras, Sir Humphrey and Jack the Lad would look on with their heads cocked and smiling. Lookout Retreat had been a happy house but it was the "big C" that eventually broke the magic. Uncle Bertie went under quickly and thankfully with little suffering. At the ripe old age of 95 it was his time. "Time," muttered Flora, "it wasn't her time yet, it was time to help Poppy to whom life hadn't been so kind and she really needed a helping hand."

Flora, being such an expert on anything to do with tea, could also read the tealeaves. Ladies from the yacht club and Uncle Bertie's golf club would gather for regular readings. Flora insisted that they came in their finery. Frieda, who helped out at one of the sea front hotels, would be hired to lay the table, prepare wafer thin sandwiches and bake a delicious assortment of cakes and scones. When Uncle Bertie was alive the tea party was rounded off with generous gin and tonics much to the ladies' delight. They were good days, Lookout Retreat, warm and welcoming, drew in the crowds and cast a soft glow over Margate.

It was the tealeaves that first warned Flora a storm was approaching. It had frightened her; Bertie had been her partner for more than 65 years. They had laughed and cried together, travelled the world, raised three children built a successful business, seen Margate flourish, decline and in more recent times climb out of the quagmire and back into the limelight. A few odd pains here and there for Bertie, far too many lengthy afternoon naps, a drastic dip in appetite signalled the beginning of the end. Now Flora was alone in a big old rambling house albeit surrounded by joyful memories, but nevertheless she was alone. They had shared a good life together. Now Sir Humphrey and Jack the Lad were old too, they might enjoy a few more years together but time was marching on.

Chapter 3

"Nothing is impossible, our dogs say so!"

One morning in one big breath Aunt Flora declared, "It's time that we visit George V1 Memorial Park, Poppy, time to visit the Italianate Greenhouse for afternoon tea and time to discuss your future! "

Poppy had already spent four weeks at Lookout Retreat. The weather had been kind, she had woken up to sunshine and warmth every day and she had regularly been riding *Dora,* Aunt Flora's old boneshaker bicycle along the cliff paths. Poppy had pedalled for miles; she loved the sea, the sand and the happy crowds who visited Margate, Broadstairs and Ramsgate on their summer holidays. She loved the brightly painted beach huts, the bucket and spade brigades, rubber tiers, inflatable dinghies, the smell of fish and chips and watching the sailing boats off the shore. The little boats reminded Poppy of her sailing days with Aunt Flora and Uncle Bertie on their yacht, *The Princess Christina.* Flora loved anything to do with royalty so she had insisted that their yacht had a royal name.

Poppy had become a familiar sight with the beach hut occupiers as she pedalled along with her bright blue floral backpack. *Dora* had a large wicker basket attached to her handlebars and Poppy had taken to scooping up Jack the Lad and taking him along. Their first venture out had been precarious; Jack the Lad didn't know what to think. He fitted nicely into the basket but it was very bumpy and felt positively dangerous. The following day Poppy had come to her senses and stuffed an old velvet cushion deep into the wicker. Jack the Lad never looked back. Riding high, nose to the wind, ears flapping and for once Flora's little Jack Russell was king of the castle and in his element. At one point, Poppy had considered acquiring a little leather helmet and goggles for him just like the Wallace and Gromit cartoon characters.

Their regular route took them through Broadstairs, down to Dumpton Gap and to Sam's bar where all the dog owners gathered for a quick cup of tea. Early morning saw an amazing number of happy dogs gathering, playing tag on the beach and splashing in the rock pools. Jack the Lad had taken on a new lease of life; things had definitely changed for the better since Poppy's arrival. Their route continued through The George V1 Memorial Park and eventually onto the cliff top at Ramsgate. Poppy loved the freedom, the wind in her hair, sea air, and the time to truly relax. For the first time in a long while she felt at peace as Margate was clearly exceeding her expectations.

Poppy particularly liked the steep ride down into the Royal Harbour at Ramsgate. This was also Aunt Flora's special place; she loved the colourful array of boats, the Royal Temple Yacht Club and afternoon tea at The Albion House Boutique Hotel perched high up on the East Cliff. Poppy personally preferred the Ship Shape Café down on the quayside under the arches, a fisherman's café with picnic tables and bright umbrellas. They did a great English cooked breakfast and Jack the Lad met up with his newly found pal, Winston, a fellow Jack Russell, cute as a button, and a regular cafe visitor. Winston received a fat juicy sausage carefully cut into bite size pieces and placed in a little white bowl for him every morning as Mary, his owner, ate her breakfast. Jack the Lad was quick to follow suit and now Ship Shape Café became a regular fixture on their morning ride. Poppy laughed at the sign perched above the tray of salt and peppershakers, brown sauce and vinegar, *"Nothing is impossible, our dogs say so!"*

Chapter 4

"Son, observe the time and fly from evil."

Yes, it was time to visit the Italianate Greenhouse and the tea garden in The George V1 Memorial Park. It was a hot, sultry afternoon in early August. Aunt Flora had dressed up. She always looked good for her 86 years, tall, slim and erect she really had good taste in clothes and would never be seen out and about without proper grooming. Today she wore an elegant floral print dress topped by a large straw hat with matching ribbons. Flora liked the genteel ambience, old wood and wrought iron chairs and tables; faded Laura Ashley printed cushions, delicious cakes and old bone china. It all met with her approval. It wasn't perfect but at least the owners had some sense of decorum. Sensible people frequented the tea garden, quiet and respectful, talking in hushed tones and Flora felt comfortably at home in this tranquil setting.

It was over a pot of Earl Grey tea and decadent chocolate fudge gateau that Aunt Flora began to speak earnestly. "Poppy dear, you cannot ride around on that old bicycle forever, do something with your life, you need a job. These days, you are looking much better, less weary. The seaside has done you a lot of good but you have to fill your days sensibly dear. We're all here to accomplish something. My grandmother once instructed me that when the time comes for me to leave this world I should be leaving it in a better place because I have been here. Poppy, look to your gifts, please don't waste time!"

Of course Aunt Flora was right, she was always right. In truth Poppy had come to Margate to heal, to find out exactly who she was and what she should be doing. Various mystics whom she had consulted over the years talked about discovering her life's purpose. Well, Poppy just didn't know what her life path and purpose was. There had been too many upsets, too many failures, too much pleasing other people, sleeping pills, antidepressants, illness and dark circles. Aunt Flora had told her once that there was no need to be sick if you were happy, happiness and fulfilment equated with good health and vitality and anyway there was nothing that couldn't be put right by the things in her medicine chest. Witch Hazel and Arnica for bumps and bruises, Chamomile Lotion for itchy skin, Milk of Magnesia for tummy upsets and if all else failed a good stiff gin and tonic! Flora never made a point of visiting the doctor; hospitals and such places were always to be avoided.

Poppy sighed; somehow Flora's life had all worked out, a lot of smooth sailing, happiness, time to dance, a loving relationship, and a successful business. She reflected upon the clock set high up on Old St Mary's Cathedral in San Francisco, *"Son, observe the time and fly from evil."* Poppy had been in the beautiful city a few years back, a work assignment had taken her there but plenty of opportunities had arisen for her to explore the city and to ride the cable cars. Each time the car had passed the clock it disturbed something deep inside, at her core. Poppy was well aware that life had taken her down paths best not trodden especially when it had come to relationships. True happiness had somehow eluded her and a hole needed fixing. Poppy just wasn't good in the fixing department and now she asked herself, "exactly why am I here in Margate and will I discover what I am looking for here?"

Chapter 5

"Keep calm and eat a cup cake."

The seafront was buzzing, it was The Margate Pride Festival and the town was decorated in its finest. Rainbow flags fluttered in the gentle breeze and there was bunting everywhere. The historic Market Place, crowded with families enjoying the recent revival in art galleries, restaurants, antique and vintage clothing, looked on benevolently happy to witness better times. Poppy stopped by at, The Curious Cup Cake Café. This was one of Aunt Flora's favourite places because they made a good cup of tea, the cakes were always fresh and to cap it all, The Queen had actually paid a visit on November 11, 2011! A lovely photograph of Her Majesty, resplendent in pink, hung close to the ordering counter and a plaque set in the wooden floorboards marked the occasion.

The Queen had come to Margate to open the new Turner Art Gallery. William Turner, 1775 – 1851, was a well-known English Romantic painter who had spent part of his life living and painting in Margate. Flora called the new art gallery, "the blot on the harbour landscape." There had been plenty of controversy leading up to the approval and final construction of The Turner Gallery but now it was well established and had surprisingly brought with it pleasant changes and fortunes to Margate's old town and the harbour area where it had been built. Old derelict buildings, all with stories to tell, had been gutted or renovated and now Margate was buzzing with visitors who brought a newfound prosperity.

Poppy settled into an old cast iron love seat outside the café. It was a very hot day and most tables were occupied. A local dance troupe was about to perform on the café's forecourt. Little girls wearing tiaras sat with their families, gay pride attendees wore rainbow cowboy hats and one lady wore a purple wig adorned with red roses. It was all rather colourful. The dance troupe warmed Poppy's heart and maybe it was their dancing, perhaps the heavy beat of the music, happy faces, or the rainbow flags but whatever it was Poppy felt a change deep within her. Today, deep in her knowing, something had shifted, something new was about to happen, August 11 was to mark an auspicious day in her life.

After tea at The Curious Cup Cake Café Poppy joined the posse of pride revellers exploring the old town heading towards the sea front ready for the parade. In all the jostling and chaos she found herself outside the Madam Popoff Vintage Emporium. Poppy looked at the ornate windows trimmed with gold paint, bygone elegance, sandwiched between King's Emporium, an eclectic mix of bric-a-brac, and an ugly scaffold clad building on the corner of King Street. The shop caught her eye. It was time to linger, time to take it all in and explore the depths of this mysterious place. "Vintage fashion is the place to be," exclaimed the glamorous shop assistant whose eccentric dress complemented the quirky façade and interior.

Bulging clothing racks had attracted a number of the fashionably young. Madam Popoff's was a veritable delight, a feast for the eyes. The shop was stuffed with shoes, handbags, evening gowns, coats, hats and gloves, glamorous accessories from days when ladies always dressed to impress. There were Victorian era wedding dresses and old lace; it was all here. Poppy wasn't exactly sure that she could or would wear any of this paraphernalia but business seemed brisk and obviously a number of customers were delighted with their newly purchased "glad rags!" Poppy liked what she saw and there was a spring in her step as she crossed the threshold back into the afternoon sun. If it had not been for a group of rowdy revellers passing at the same time Poppy would even have missed the small card placed in one of the large windows.

"Part time help required. Only special people need apply."

Chapter 6

Poppy had cycled down to old Margate with Jack the Lad. It was early morning and she was sitting on the harbour arm wall by the sculpture of Mrs. Booth the shell lady, who had been William Turner's mistress. From this good position Poppy could see across to the Margate seafront. The corner of King Street, with its scaffold clad White Hart Mansions building, prominent in its ugliness, competed with The Turner Gallery, Aunt Flora's, "blot on the landscape." A stone's throw from the corner of King Street was The Old Kent Market: which entrepreneurs had painted a garish lobster pink. Poppy fondly recalled the time it was an old cinema and how when she was very young Uncle Bertie had taken her to see the high adventure movie *King Solomon's Mines,* "It's funny how you remember such odd things," Poppy muttered to herself.

Margate Clock Tower striking 8am interrupted her reminiscences. "Time," murmured Poppy, "yes, it is time to act." Poppy hadn't been able to put the small card in Madam Popoff's window out of her mind. What disturbed her most was the fact that only special people need apply. "How audacious, who does Madam Popoff think she is?" Poppy asked Jack the Lad.

Under Poppy's puzzlement was a deeply rooted anxiety. Poppy didn't know if she was special, certainly the circumstances of her life hadn't been remarkable in any way. Poppy had always worked hard and tried her best to please people. She was honest, responsible, neat and tidy, efficient, always a reliable personal assistant but special? She never considered herself special. People had taken advantage of her good nature, some had excluded her from their inner circles, and others had looked down upon her. Poppy had never managed to figure out people or what she was doing wrong. She had a string of failed relationships behind her and bitter disappointments caused a huge dent to form in her self worth.

Jack the Lad, head cocked, listened and waited patiently. He knew that Poppy was upset and ill at ease but he couldn't stop thinking about Winston and the fat sausages waiting for him at Ship Shape Café. Poppy gathered him into the wicker basket and they set off for Ramsgate, which is where Poppy found solace in the jaunty sign above the brown sauce.

"Nothing is impossible, our dogs say so!"

Chapter 7

"To dress and to mend the broken pieces."

Some days later Poppy and Aunt Flora were at the dressmakers. Flora was having the final fitting for her matching dress and bolero jacket, and everything had to be ready and perfect for the forthcoming Lord Mayor's charity cream tea at The Italianate Greenhouse. Flora's friends would be there, those who were left and hadn't fallen off the perch, as Uncle Bertie had always described the passing of a fellow traveller. Old, elegant ladies, from another era, respectable, proper, gathering to take proper tea out of fine bone china cups and while away a few hours with refined small talk.

Poppy suddenly jumped up and exclaimed, "Enough, I need to do something, I'll see you back at Lookout Retreat later today!" With a burst of energy she was gone. Flora and her dressmaker watched as Poppy ran down the path, through the gate and scurried towards the bus stop. Flora's eyes rolled as she remarked, "Young people these days!"

Poppy was on a mission, Madam Popoff was beckoning, a deep force, almost like a magnet had somehow grabbed at Poppy's inner being and she also found the urge to be forceful. It was time to make a business call, meet Madam herself, discuss the part time employment opportunity and begin to live. Poppy had acquired a newly discovered confidence and decided that at least she could pretend to be special and entice Madam Popoff into giving her a job.

As Poppy entered, Isadora, the rather eccentric looking shop assistant, smiled. "Good afternoon I'm Poppy and I would like a word with Madam Popoff please." Hearing her name a little roly-poly of a woman, her face was wizened with age appeared from behind a large costume mirror in the corner of the establishment announcing, "I am She."

It had become increasingly clear that during their time together nobody could fool Madam. She had crystal blue all seeing eyes. She had seen it all, Poppy's pain, her anger and her fears, lack of self-confidence and poor sense of self worth. Madam had kindly taken Poppy's hand and whispered, "Poppy dear, you will find healing here, lessons will be learnt, dark holes sealed, where there is fear and anger, you will find love, where there is hate you will find forgiveness, where there is misery, joy."

Madam had shared how all kinds of people came to her shop, some to browse, some to purchase, some to steal, some to simply find refuge from the hot sun or the rain and cold weather. She also explained that most important of all were those that came to heal because her mission in life was two fold, *to dress and to mend the broken pieces.*

As Poppy gathered up her things to leave, Madam Popoff called out, "Please begin on Thursday, 11am sharp. My rule is that you come every day with an open mind, and remember Poppy you have a proper home here. I've been waiting for you to call."

Poppy wasn't really sure exactly what happened next. Time seemed to be playing tricks on her. When she finally glanced down at her wristwatch ready to return to Lookout Retreat she had been there for the best part of three hours. "How extraordinary," Poppy muttered to herself, "three hours! Waiting for me," Poppy repeated the words out loud. Margate was proving to be a most mysterious and exotic place.

Later that week Flora and Poppy were riding around on the number 69 open top bus. It always attracted the crowds of summer visitors in its smart cream livery. The local bus company provided open top rides around the coast during the summer months and Aunt Flora loved to pass away the time up top with a bird's eye view of all the local happenings. She could peer into gardens otherwise obscured by high walls and hedges. It was Folk Week in Broadstairs and today the bus afforded a very good view of all the various comings and goings of this lively annual festival by the sea. Since the 1960's Folk Week always attracted large crowds of talented musicians, dancers and onlookers mostly clothed in merry costumes trimmed with bells. Morris men and women danced in the streets, along the sea front walk and at the bandstand. Whoops of delight could be heard as Clarence, the Dragon and the Hooden Horses entertained hordes of people. Folk Week was a particularly happy occasion. Ice creams, laughing, singing, dancing, the craft fair and quaint Broadstairs, its picturesque harbour, the sun and the sand all created the ambience. Flora absolutely loved the dancing and insisted upon wearing a garland of flowers and ribbons around her silver hair, making her look just like a gay young girl again.

Poppy was not so happy; she had butterflies in her tummy. Tomorrow was the day Madam Popoff had commanded her to make an appearance at 11am, sharp. All her life Poppy had dithered. She found it difficult to make up her mind and now she was wondering if her visit to the Madam Popoff Vintage Emporium had been the wisest of choices. Aunt Flora sensed her mounting anxiety and exclaimed, "Poppy dear, this will be an adventure, you will meet new people, pull yourself together and take courage. Action fuels a better tomorrow!"

Well, Poppy did pluck up enough courage the next day to present herself on time and it all proved to be the beginning of something quite wonderful, even magical. Isadora was absolutely delightful, her warm heart shone through the eccentric clothes and the outrageous headpieces that she frequently wore. They complemented the racks of costumes that the fashionably young liked to sift through.

Isadora took Poppy under her wing. After a few weeks Poppy felt fully established at the vintage emporium. Local residents, spring-cleaning closets and attics, would often drop off bags of clothes on the doorstep and Madam would occasionally leave and go on hunting expeditions further afield in search of suitable merchandise for the store. Madam would say, "The older the better and certainly anything older than 1980 would do." Poppy would help to sort, price and display besides making pleasant, small talk with customers. She enjoyed the company and the quirky ambience of the shop. It was all very different and a refreshing change from the stuffy London office where she had spent most of her working life. The 11 am start still gave her time to do her early morning cliff top bicycle ride with Jack the Lad and there was still plenty of time to breakfast at Ship Shape Café and meet up with Winston for sausages.

Madam Popoff had strange habits. Poppy, growing in confidence, had become more observant of these. As the weeks flew by Poppy began to notice that Madam would carefully feel the things that crossed the threshold of her establishment and smile, but on more than one occasion Poppy saw looks of abject horror and once Madam even fainted. Poppy didn't know what to make of this strange behaviour. After all the establishment's stock were merely old clothes, shoes, bags, hats and other paraphernalia. Poppy's growing curiosity prompted her to think about asking some questions. "There's a lot more going on here than meets the eye," Poppy whispered to herself.

Madam had sensed Poppy's concern and one day when the shop was quiet she took her aside for a long and serious chat. "Poppy dear, everything has energy, these clothes, shoes, hats, gloves, bags, costume jewels all belonged to someone. They are part of that person's story. We all have stories to tell, some are happy but others are sad, desperate even. We offer a costume service Poppy, customers like our second hand offerings. When they come here and find something special they are generally very happy and take their treasures home with a sense of satisfaction, thrill even. I also view myself as a gatekeeper. I won't allow anything to leave here that can seriously disturb their peace of mind. Festering, dark energies can and do attach themselves. I provide a quality control service. My well developed and honed sensitivity is like a radar, it will help me decide what stays on the racks and shelves waiting for a new owner and what must be packed up straight away and dispatched as soon as possible to the bonfire at my allotment garden. Some lives are so cruel Poppy, hard, so ugly that they leave an evil stamp. I can feel such things through my touch and I know that fire is the only answer, a sort of spiritual cleansing, so into the fire they go never to be used again."

Gate keeper, honed sensitivity, evil energies, Poppy reflected. Now she needed "thinking time," as Uncle Bertie used to say. Such possibilities had never crossed her mind before; she thought that surely they were all just old clothes and accessories. However, she did know that the Madam Popoff Vintage Emporium was a happy place to work just like Lookout Retreat. Both places felt warm, welcoming and joyful and Poppy did know that there were many places she had visited in London and on her travels to foreign parts that didn't feel so good. They felt dark and creepy and the only thing to do was to get out and run. The image of the clock on Old St Mary's Cathedral, in San Francisco, suddenly flashed through her mind, *"Son, observe the time and fly from evil."*

"Fly from evil," Poppy muttered to herself. She was here to learn lessons; Madam Popoff was providing wise counsel and Poppy began to pay attention to her hands, her long slender fingers and the old things that she handled.

Chapter 8

Madam Popoff was away on one of her hunting expeditions and Isadora had telephoned Poppy in the early morning announcing she would have to stay home today and care for her sister's little boy who wasn't well. It was September 5th, a warm, sunny day but quieter than usual because the children had just returned to school for the new academic year. The crowds of holiday visitors had dwindled and retired folk on bargain breaks now frequented the old town and seafront.

A battered cardboard box waited to be discovered on the doorstep as Margate Clock Tower struck 11am and Poppy used the big iron key to open the shop door. She flipped the sign over to OPEN and picked up the box. It was heavy with a neat luggage tag instructing the finder to please give the contents a very good home. Poppy carefully opened the box and fingered through the contents. A musty smell spilled out into the shop. At the bottom of the box Poppy discovered a treasure. She carefully placed it on the oak counter top and went into the back room to make herself a cup of coffee. When she returned she sat down and spent some time carefully examining the treasure. It was a beautiful beaded clutch purse with an old fashioned clasp. It looked Art Deco, perhaps circa 1920 – 1930. The tiny beads, colourful hues of emerald green, striking blues and purple, made a beautiful image of irises blowing in the wind. The whole bag was exquisite. Poppy clutched it with both hands, drew it closer and rested it upon her heart; she closed her eyes and was suddenly taken back to, another time.

It was September 5th, 1925 and Lady Southborough stood in the lifeboat house at the end of the Margate Jetty. She had dressed for the occasion, resplendent in a beautiful emerald and blue suit, matching feathered hat and held a lovely new clutch purse decorated with fine beads that made a design of irises blowing in the wind. The new bag had been a special birthday present from her husband. Lord Southborough was chairman of,

The Civil Service Lifeboat Fund, and today she had been invited to name the new Margate motor lifeboat, *The Lord Southborough*. As she swung the bottle of champagne against the hull she declared, "May God bless all who sail in her." What a joyous occasion for Margate, a new lifeboat, and the first one to be powered by an engine. The lifeboat had always been most important to a community whose many inhabitants depended upon the sea to provide their livelihood. Margate harbour was crowded with an assortment of boats mainly those belonging to fishermen and the local men looked to the lifeboat when bad weather caught them off guard and they desperately needed help.

Poppy smiled as she opened her eyes, she had smelt the salty sea air, heard the gulls wheeling overhead, felt the sun and wind on her face and the sense of joy and expectation. Above all she had shared the deep gratitude of the Margate people who had gathered that day by the water to applaud and welcome their new boat. Today, September 5th, both then and now was a good day, one that warmed Poppy's heart.

Poppy had no more time to reflect as a group of elderly ladies, on a day trip crossed the threshold and kept her busy. When she finally turned the sign to CLOSED around 4 o'clock, Poppy decided to stop by the lifeboat house on the harbour quayside on her ride back home. She had never been in the lifeboat house before; she walked around *Leonard Kent*, the present Mersey Class Lifeboat and browsed the walls filled with old photographs and articles documenting Margate's long association with lifeboats beginning in 1860.

As she stepped back out into the September sunshine her gaze took her across the quayside to the sea and the sculpture by Antony Gormley of a lone man standing on an old concreted area where Margate's Jetty had once stood. The man, gazing out to sea, called *Another Time*, struck a chord in Poppy's heart. Earlier this day an exquisite bag had transported her back to this very day in 1925. The seascape had been so different then, a busy jetty, a lifeboat house and steep slip at the jetty's end, a harbour filled with boats and fishermen, a community happy and deeply appreciative, in another time!

The next day with Madam Popoff still being absent and Isadora away looking after her sister's son, Poppy had more time for reflection. Since the shop was quiet Poppy once again made herself a cup of coffee and settled down to contemplate how much money she should write on the sales tag for the new treasure. Poppy examined the exquisite beadwork creating the beautiful image of irises and turned the bag gently in her hands, and then she opened the old fashioned clasp. Emerald green silk lined the interior and out fell an old photograph. Poppy held it closer so that she could clearly see the image of a young soldier. She turned it over and read the brief message on the back.

"Iris, words aren't enough to thank you, a piece of my heart will always remain in Margate with you and with all those who saved my life. May you always be blessed."

Harry – Christmas 1940

Poppy gently placed the faded photograph on her heart, she closed her eyes and once again she was transported back to another time, it was the summer of 1940.

They called the evacuation of 338,226 allied soldiers, *The Miracle of Dunkirk* as desperate men were plucked from the beaches and harbour mole of Dunkirk between May 26 and June 04, 1940. Large numbers of troops had been cut off and surrounded by German troops during the six week long, *Battle of Britain.* Prime Minister, Winston Churchill, had called it, "a colossal military disaster." A large section of the British Army had been stranded at Dunkirk. The huge operation mounted to facilitate their rescue involved 39 British Royal Navy destroyers, four Royal Canadian destroyers and a variety of civilian merchant ships. Many soldiers had to wade out into shoulder deep water and wait patiently until it was their turn to be ferried to the larger ships by a manoeuvre that came to be known as, *The Little Ships of Dunkirk.* The flotilla of hundreds of merchant marine boats, fishing boats, pleasure craft, yachts and two lifeboats had all been called into service to help save the men.

Harry, a young Canadian soldier, had been badly wounded by machine gun fire. He was a fine soldier, greatly loved by his fellow service men, and now they vowed that they would do their best to ensure that he got onto one of the boats and be whisked to safety. Margate men had bravely answered Churchill's clarion call and many small boats ventured out from the safety of the harbour. *The Lord Southborough* was one of two lifeboats that made numerous trips across the channel. It rescued over 600 soldiers whilst under fire from German bombers and having to navigate the dangerous waters infested with mines. Altogether 49,342 soldiers were landed in Margate. Townspeople rallied as the injured, sick and starving were carried into seafront hotels and pubs. The locals brought food, water and warm clothing and did the best that they could to provide refuge and comfort before those that were able to could march to the railway station and journey on to London.

Young Harry had been lifted onto *The Lord Southborough* but when he arrived ashore he was barely conscious. His legs had been badly injured and breathing through the pain was all that he could muster. Kind Margate men gently lifted him onto one of Pettman's fleet of vehicles and he was taken to nearby Margate General Hospital.

On June 2nd, the same day that Harry was being whisked to the hospital, a young girl called Margaret, her big sister, Iris, and their mother set out for Margate railway station. Margaret was fifteen years. It was a beautiful hot June day and today was the day when she was to be evacuated with her school, Clarendon House, en masse with loads of other children. She carried a small suitcase, a tag and a gas mask. There was chaos in Margate. As they made their way to the station they witnessed long lines of ambulances stretching all the way along St Peter's Road where they lived. Once the family arrived at the station they had to clamber over many of the soldiers, as they lay injured or exhausted on the station steps. Some didn't even have their uniforms left they were just in long john underwear. Some were terribly injured. It was a sad and very fearful day for Margaret as she stood on the platform and hugged her big sister and mother goodbye.

Iris was barely twenty years old and had been nursing for a couple of years, now her skills and compassion were needed more than ever. She left the station and hurried towards the hospital. At the door she hastily adjusted her cap and apron and checked her watch. The past few days had been a nightmare, she had seen such horrific injuries as she had dressed wounds and had gently held the hands of brave young men who had taken their last breath. It was noon when she heard a young man called Harry screaming with pain in the hospital ward. Sister had asked Iris to do what she could before a doctor could get to him. This was to herald the beginning of a deep and personal friendship as Iris continued to nurse him for the many months that followed. She sat by his bedside when the ward was less busy, generally late at night. She heard about his family back in Canada, his parent's farm, his big sister who was also nursing at a Toronto hospital and all about his childhood sweetheart, Mavis.

It was the loving care and support of Iris, together with the other nursing staff and the skill of the doctors that saved Harry's life. He was also extremely grateful to the older ladies of nearby St John's Church who would take turns to volunteer and visit with the critically ill soldiers. The ladies reminded the soldiers of their own mothers who waited anxiously for news.

As Christmas 1940 approached Margate Hospital announced that there would be a Christmas dance for all the staff and their guests. Harry, now about to be discharged, joked with Iris asking who was going to take her to the ball. Iris blushed, she had been so busy working that there had been no time to step out with any suitable young men. Harry was just able to get down on one knee as he asked if Iris might accompany him to the ball. He was due to leave town the day afterwards and he felt that the hospital ball would appropriately mark his parting farewell to Iris and celebrate the passage of time he had spent in the warm loving embrace of Margate and its people.

Iris returned home all flustered and complained to her mother that she had absolutely nothing that she could wear. Several conversations later with some of the ladies from St John's Church finally provided the answer.

The next day a carefully wrapped package arrived on her doorstep. Iris eagerly unwrapped the thick brown paper tied with string and out bounced a beautiful white layered chiffon gown speckled with tiny royal blue polka dots. The gown came with a matching wrap and the most exquisite clutch bag decorated with irises blowing in the wind and all made from tiny beads.

"Oh, my!" Exclaimed Iris and her mum in unison as they read the accompanying message written on a brown luggage label:

"Iris dear, you have given much. I once worked as Lady Southborough's lady's maid, she passed this lovely ball gown and bag onto me a few years ago and asked that I might one day find them a suitable home. Enjoy the ball Iris and thank you."

Iris and Harry made a delightful couple and after such a happy evening it was hard to say goodbye but Harry knew his family and his sweetheart were waiting patiently across the ocean. Harry slipped his photo into her purse as they bade farewell. They never saw each other again. Iris eventually met a wonderful Margate man, Harry married Mavis, had a family of his own and lived through to a grand old age. His life had been blessed with lots of good fortune but he never forgot Margate and the men who had risked their own lives to pluck him from the beaches of Dunkirk and he always remembered the young nurse who had held his hand through his darkest moments of fear and pain. As Harry's own time had drawn nearer he had taken aside his oldest daughter and requested that when he passed away would she please ensure that a bouquet of irises adorn his coffin, there was to be nothing else. He never explained why but insisted that she keep her promise.

Poppy opened her eyes, she had been crying, she looked at her watch, a whole hour had passed away. "Another time," she muttered as she lovingly examined again the beautiful clutch bag with the iris design and the photograph of the young soldier.

Chapter 9

Poppy was sitting outside Mala Kaffe on the harbour arm. The late afternoon sun lit up her face as Margate Clock Tower struck 4.30 pm. She looked across the harbour, the tide was out, fishing boats keeled to their side in the mud and there was a rank smell of seaweed as the gulls overhead wheeled. Poppy looked up towards The Turner Gallery, Aunt Flora's, "blot on the landscape," Margate Lifeboat Station and behind them all, up on Fort Hill, the partly obscured Arcadian Building. This had been a public house and hotel in 1940 and was where many of the wounded Dunkirk men had been taken as they were carried from the boats that tied up at the Margate Jetty. A young waitress brought a fancy glass pot of green tea and a glass all set nicely out on a wooden IKEA tray. Poppy inquired if the café had once been a fisherman's storage shed. "I don't really know," she replied. "I come from Australia and I've only been in Margate three months."

Poppy watched the little green balls of fine jasmine tea gradually open out like a lotus flower greeting the sun. As she poured the delicate green tinted water into her glass she contemplated the happenings of the past few months. Poppy had also only been in Margate for barely three months but the town and its history was already resting comfortably in her heart.

She loved and coveted the exquisite bag with the beaded iris design. However, necessity dictated that she should set a price, so at twenty pounds it sat regally on a shelf of its own. Really the bag was priceless, Poppy knew it and so did Madam Popoff. Poppy wanted more than anything to buy it and take it home with her to Lookout Retreat. Knowing this, earlier that day, Madam had taken her into the back room and reprimanded her.

"Poppy dear, you want to buy that bag, I know it! Everyday your eyes tell me so. It's a beautiful bag but it doesn't have your name written on it!"

Poppy looked at her questioningly, "Sometimes in life, Poppy, there are things that we want, things that we can well afford to buy, things that we fall in love with, but actually they don't belong to us. We don't deserve them. More to the point, Poppy, they won't be happy with us! Things, like people, take on a life of their own and they have energy. That bag belongs to the lifeboat community." Poppy's eyes widened in wonder as Madam continued. "Everything is connected, and that bag has a connection with lifeboats, more specifically to *The Lord Southborough*, a young soldier and a nurse called Iris." As Poppy listened she now understood that Madam Popoff really did know everything.

"The bag belongs to one of the stalwart ladies who stand for hours in rain or shine or who knock on doors during lifeboat fundraising week. Raising money from public contributions is vital if new boats are to be purchased, older ones maintained and then there's the station's running costs. It belongs to the gift shop volunteers and to the wives, daughters and other family members of the men who man the lifeboats and risk their own lives to save those who probably should have known better, listened to the weather forecast and stayed home that day! Right now that bag has been entrusted to us for safekeeping. It will remain on our shelf and one day, sometime in the future, a special person will cross over our threshold. The bag will become their treasure; it will be ready to begin a new story in another time. That special person will have rightful ownership because they will belong to the wider lifeboat family. They will choose the bag and more importantly, Poppy, the exquisite iris bag will have chosen them!"

Poppy had ventured to Margate to learn life's lessons. She had never before entertained the idea that things had an energy, either good or bad, depending on their ownership and more to the point, things had rightful ownership. There were some things that belonged to us and other things that were best left alone. Poppy looked down at her long delicate fingers. She had learnt to use her hands and was beginning to feel her way through life in a different way, a better way. She was beginning to understand life's mysteries and the unseen threads that connect people, places and their lives both now, in the past and even in the future. There were times, such as Dunkirk, that Poppy never witnessed because she was not yet born and times in the future that she would never see because her time had already passed.

Poppy began to recall Aunt Flora's words spoken a few months back at The Italianate Greenhouse. "My grandmother once instructed me that when the time comes I should be leaving the world a better place because I was here. Poppy look to your gifts and above all, don't waste time!"

Chapter 10

As the weeks passed by the weather became much colder and the old town visitors dwindled significantly. Madam Popoff's Vintage Emporium had become very quiet so Madam, Isadora and Poppy put their heads together in a brainstorming session. How to attract more customers into the shop was top of their agenda, Madam also wanted to provide a place where the elderly town residents could gather over a cuppa, share stories and company. There were so many lonely people shut up in their homes over the winter months desperate for company. "We are herd animals," Madam announced, "how can we tempt them in here?"

Poppy suggested chocolate cake, "Everyone loves chocolate, and it brings people together." No one wanted to take away business from the local cafes so it was mutually decided to offer a cuppa and homemade cake for a pound and all proceeds would be donated to charity. Those who attended Madam's gatherings could vote for their favourite charity and a new charity was to be picked each week. It was decided that Tuesday and Friday mornings 11- 1pm during the winter months would be a fine time to gather. Poppy and Isadora agreed to provide two homemade chocolate cakes each every week and Madam would provide the drinks.

Poppy was to be dispatched out and about to locate and purchase old china tea services and Isadora came up with the sewing machine table idea. "We are a costume emporium, we can find some old Singer sewing machine tables to sit around, I've seen these things when I was on holiday in America, new restaurants made to look old." Madam smiled and patted Isadora on the back, "How clever! Poppy please add those to your shopping list along with some appropriate chairs to match."

A few days later Poppy found herself in Scott's Furniture Mart, an establishment founded in 1969 with 16,000 square feet to explore. The colourful flier announced, "An Aladdin's cave of three floors two yards and various warehouses full of furniture, antiques, architectural salvage, bygones and everything old fashioned." Scott's is situated at The Old Ice Works in Bath Place, a stone's throw from the neighbouring Shell Grotto. Not only was it a feast for the eyes but also Poppy found it extremely difficult to navigate her way through the maze of memorabilia, old furniture and bygone treasures. The old Singer sewing machine tables huddled together in a dusty corner away from the visitor's well-trodden path. Three tables were in very good condition and Poppy struck up a bargain deal with the proprietor. "Not much call for this sort of thing these days," he remarked as he took Poppy's handful of cash then he winked his eye and tipped his cloth cap. "Of course I am always happy to oblige Madam Popoff, please tell her that I said hello."

A couple of burly men were summoned to help Poppy load a small van that she had hired from, B & Q DIY Store. The sewing machine tables were loaded in first then the assortment of a dozen old wooden chairs. None of them matched but Poppy felt quite confident that everything would look good in Madam's already quirky shop.

Clothing racks were pushed aside and the sewing machine tables manoeuvred into place. Each table had four chairs and it all created a cosy picture. Madam decided that they should all be stored in the back room after her morning soirees. Poppy had amassed a collection of nice bone china; all mismatched odds and ends from Margate Old Town shopping emporiums. Word spread quickly in the community that Madam Popoff was venturing into the entertainment business and Ollie, ancient but nevertheless a very accomplished harpist, asked if he could come and play his harp on Tuesday and Friday mornings. Ollie had been an orchestra man for over 60 years but his failing memory and shaky hands had put an end to an otherwise stellar career. Madam had gently taken his frail hands and smiled, "Of course, Ollie, you and your heavenly harp will always be welcome here."

A trial run was planned for Sunday afternoon. Aunt Flora, Isadora's extended family and a few Margate Old Town neighbours were invited just to see if a harp, cuppa and a cake would all actually work in the store.

Flora came along with Sir Humphrey and Jack the Lad in tow, She liked the bone china and the harpist but suggested that a few nice tablecloths might complete the picture. Flora also volunteered to come in and read the tealeaves; this had always drawn a crowd amongst her friends, the yacht club ladies and those from Bertie's golf club. Madam smiled as their plan was coming nicely together.

Poppy recalled seeing old tablecloths in the same battered brown box that she had discovered the exquisite bag with the beaded iris flowers blowing in the wind. She looked up wistfully at the shelf where the elegant bag had been regally placed. No one had come in for it yet.

Poppy opened the battered old cardboard box and pulled out several small linen tablecloths, they had been carefully folded and were ideal for a small tea table. These would be most suitable. The carefully embroidered flower designs were quite lovely. Poppy took them over to Madam and exclaimed, "These were lovingly made by a lady quite expert in the art of needlework and making beautiful things!" Madam took the tablecloths from Poppy, gently held them, and as she did so she began to cry. "Poppy dear, never make assumptions, these beautiful tablecloths were made by a gentleman."

The following day Poppy had the shop all to herself. Madam was away on another hunting expedition and Isadora had taken the day off to help her sister with her nephew's birthday party planned for after school. After a general tidy up as Poppy settled down with a cup of coffee and the newspaper she remembered the tablecloths and Madam's sudden outburst of grief. It was raining heavily and Margate was particularly quiet. There had been no customers since she opened up the shop. Poppy pulled the beautiful tablecloths out of the box and fingered them gently admiring the carefully stitched floral designs. She was particularly attracted to the one with bright red poppies, her namesake. She pulled it closer, rested it on her heart, closed her eyes, and once again she was transported back to another time.

It was 1950, Margate was still recovering from the trauma of war, and food was still subject to rationing. Petrol rationing, first imposed at the onset of the war, now continued five years afterwards. It had become a hotly debated issue during the general election campaign of that year.

A dashing army captain, returning from active duty in Palestine during the mandate, had married his sweetheart in June of 1948. The couple visited Margate on their honeymoon, loved it so much that they had decided to make it their home. Dennis and Lily spent all their savings on a big old Georgian house in Margate and for almost two years now they had worked together on its renovation. Lily wasn't sure if the plaster's dust, hard work or the ill effects of the war had brought it all on she didn't understand sickness, but she knew her darling Dennis was very sick.

It had all begun with a cough that didn't go away, chest pain, then growing fatigue, chills, fever and night sweats. When Lily noticed blood on his crisp white cotton handkerchiefs she finally insisted that Dennis visit the doctor. The diagnosis had been very grim. Dennis had active Tuberculosis. It wasn't looking good for him as his right lung had been badly affected and he would need an operation immediately. Money was tight; the young couple had converted their big old house into flats that were currently occupied by American service personnel and their families who were based at nearby Manston Airfield.

Streptomycin, the first antibiotic to treat active TB, had been introduced in 1946 so Dennis was going to receive this new treatment along with pioneering thoracic surgery at The Royal Brompton Hospital in London. This was a specialist heart and lung hospital where the surgeons were instrumental in the development of advanced surgical techniques. The few months that Dennis spent up in the hospital had been agonizing. It had been hit or miss for a long time, he was desperately ill and Lily could only take the train from Margate and visit him once a week on a Sunday. They had discussed so many dreams for their future that she just couldn't let him go and it was Lily's unfailing love that kept Dennis alive.

When he was well enough to leave London, his doctors wanted him to continue his recovery at the sanatorium in Ashford, Kent. Lily decided to visit The Royal Sea Bathing Hospital in Westbrook. After all this hospital was on their doorstep and had a long and distinguished history connected with the care of TB. When Lily arrived she was told that they did not cater for those suffering from pulmonary TB. Lily's hospital visit caused her a great deal of concern and fear. She felt that Dennis had a better chance of survival and of complete recovery if he was away from other critically sick people. Isolation would be his best chance and she was determined not to lose her prince.

"Prince and Princess," had been the best description for the once glamorous couple who had always been so happy, and had been the life and the soul of any party. Lily's friends had described her as, "champagne." Now Dennis cut a pitiful image as he alighted the Margate train. He was so relieved to be home, the fresh sea air greeted him and the warm June sunshine lit up his sunken face. Lily held his arm as he walked very slowly to the waiting cab. The military man, once so strong and vital, was a mere shadow of his former self. Tuberculosis robbed him of his dignity and of his light that had once upon a time burnt so brightly, now it was ever so dim and flickering.

It was in such adversity that Lily gained the strength to hold them both up. Her darling Dennis had made it through the surgery and the critical months that had followed and now she would nurse him through the very long road back to health. TB was such a taboo subject. People were frightened when they heard that word and quite rightfully so. It was a dreadful disease. Lily had a boarding house to run, it was their livelihood, telling her tenants that her husband had TB was impossible. She would simply have to tell them all a lie. When they asked she simply said, "My husband's brain was injured in the war and he's not able to be in the house."

Lily spent weeks before his homecoming scrubbing out the old brick shed in their garden. She whitewashed the plaster walls, placed brightly coloured rugs on the concrete floor and found some old framed prints from the junk shop to decorate the walls. Fred, the kindly neighbour from next door, helped Lily to move a single bed, lamp table and comfortable armchair into the small brick building. The hermitage was now ready to welcome her beau.

It was two years before Dennis was ready to fully resume life, ready to enter the big house, to begin where he had once left off. The passage of time spent in the brick garden shed had been long and very lonely. He had plenty of thinking time and of course there was the radio and lots of books and magazines to read but Dennis needed more to occupy himself. Lily sat patiently with him at his bedside and taught him how to sew and thus it was that he came to carefully create the most beautiful tablecloths, a testament to Lily's care and all encompassing love. When the sun shone and it was warm; the shed door and window were opened and Dennis watched the birds in the garden and the colourful flowers blowing in the breeze. He listened to the gulls wheeling overhead and to the hens and rooster at the bottom of the garden. His fingers made things of beauty far removed from his desperate disease, the trauma and the loss that he had witnessed as a soldier in the war and during the mandate in Palestine.

The tablecloths were his true healer. His sewing needles and the brightly coloured threads transformed all the darker energies that had infiltrated his mind and body into the energy of beauty and forgiveness. Dennis learnt to let go of all the bad things that had passed and in doing so he had opened up room in his heart and soul for new possibilities. The passage of time brought the gift of grace and wisdom, understanding of life's miracles and an understanding that if you have enough love then anything is possible. Dennis was ready to begin again.

Poppy was crying as she heard Madam's words again in her mind. "Poppy dear, never make assumptions, these beautiful tablecloths were made by a gentleman." She opened her eyes and looked lovingly down at the carefully folded linen cloths, she knew their story and she was beginning to understand a lot more about life and how people truly heal. Poppy knew these tablecloths would be just perfect for the old Singer tables as

Madam's guests would sip their cuppa, eat chocolate cake and listen to Ollie's heavenly harp.

Chapter 11

Madam's soirees were a huge success, word had spread quickly and several local charities benefited from the generous donations made by grateful members of the senior community. Many came to hear Ollie's heavenly harp but the chocolate cake seemed to win first place amongst most people's affections. Isadora shared the recipe with her sister who kindly rolled up her sleeves and produced two extra cakes each week much to Poppy's relief. Takings at the till increased as more elderly ladies began to reminiscence and swoon over Madam's eclectic mix of paraphernalia.

Madam encouraged them to try her hats on whilst they sipped their tea and once on many were most reluctant to part with their bygone treasures. Poppy's linen tablecloths added extra beauty and ambience to the whole event and Aunt Flora enjoyed the extra limelight as she read the tealeaves of the adventurous and the curious.

Christmas was approaching fast when Poppy opened up early one morning. There had been a hint of snow in the air as she had cycled down Fort Hill, the harbour was cold, grey and uninviting as heavy, dark clouds rolled in from the sea. A large black bin liner had been left propped up against the shop door with a hastily scribbled note requesting that Madam may find the enclosed useful.

Poppy switched on the lights and the portable radiators and ran into the back room to make herself a cup of coffee. Once she was settled and feeling warmer she began to examine the contents of the bin liner. There were a few old coats and dresses probably from around 1960 and although they were all in good condition there was nothing remarkable. Poppy began to dig a little deeper and discovered a large old cardboard box and much to her delight it was filled with treasures. It was a box full of shiny

Christmas ornaments, probably from the 1950's – 1960's, lovely glass baubles and miniature gingerbread houses.

"Oh!" Exclaimed Poppy, "this is going to be a much better day than I had anticipated." Poppy wanted to decorate Madam's large picture windows for the Christmas season. After all many shopkeepers had made the effort. She visualized a lovely tree in the window adorned with her newly found treasures and some brightly wrapped boxes scattered around the base. She could even visualize some fairy lights. "I can pick those up from B & Q," she muttered to herself.

Poppy failed to notice the little knitted Superman doll until the black bag had been emptied and carefully folded and the old coats and dresses hung up on Madam's already bulging racks. He was about one foot tall and somewhat faded but nevertheless a jaunty little fellow with his bright red cape and his smiling face. Poppy sat back down, with no customers in the shop and being quite alone she held him close to her heart, closed her eyes and yet again she was transported back to, another time.

Since the 1950's and 1960's Margate had become quite the holiday and day-tripper destination. Happy families arrived on the train and headed to Margate sands for a welcome break. Mainly it was, "those down from London." Alf was a London cabbie, a big, burly, no nonsense sort of man, "salt of the earth," his friends would say. He had fought for his country during the war; and was one of the lucky young men plucked from the Dunkirk beaches relatively unscathed. There was a special place in his heart for Margate men who had risked their lives to bring him back. He enjoyed returning to the town several times each year, eating fish and chips out of the local newspaper and jellied eels from Manning's Seafood Stall on the Margate harbour slipway.

Alf lived in the East End of London and knew all the roads in the big city like, "the back of his hand." He was popular with all the other cabbies and was eager to support *The Albany Taxi Charity*; the cabbies had met at premises in Albany Road and arranged the first London Licensed Taxi Drivers outing for special needs children and their caretakers to Margate.

The year was 1972 and 36 brightly decorated taxicabs left London with 72 children and their helpers. Alf really enjoyed decorating his black taxicab and getting in a supply of sweets and other goodies for the youngsters.

It was a lovely hot day in Margate as Alf's brood spilled out onto the Margate seafront, buckets and spades in hand. The helpers had bulging picnic baskets and Alf arranged to meet them on the sand by The Sundeck once he had parked his cab and had a quick cup of tea. It was after Alf had pulled into the Margate Station Car Park and had finished chatting with some fellow cabbies that he noticed a jaunty Superman knitted doll leaning upright on his back seat. Alf took him to the café and then onto Margate sands thinking that one of his brood had left him behind. However, much to his surprise no one claimed him. "Where has the super hero come from?" Alf asked his little band of excited children but no one had a clue and the little knitted doll, just like the comic book superhero character, proved to be an enigma.

Excited children who needed watching distracted Alf so for the remainder of the morning and the early afternoon he was busy playing in the water, building sandcastles, passing out the picnic lunch and queuing up for ice creams. As Margate Clock Tower struck three o' clock his happy brood headed up onto the promenade and towards Dreamland Amusement Park with their helpers.

Alf breathed a sigh of relief he now had a few hours to himself. In more recent years when Alf and his wife had visited Margate he spent some time visiting the children at The Royal Sea Bathing Hospital. It was a short walk along Margate seafront to Westbrook and Alf had always been grateful to the staff that had nursed his comrades back in 1940. This hospital had acted as a Casualty Clearing Station during May and June of 1940 and some 400 wounded military personnel had received their primary treatment there.

Alf liked to visit Armstrong Ward where the sick boys were nursed. The hospital had always been associated with non-pulmonary TB patients but in more recent times they had taken in those requiring specialist long-term orthopaedic care. Alf knew that many of the children were resident for many months; he liked to visit, tell them stories, cheer them up and pass out little bags of chocolate when the ward sister wasn't looking. He had quite forgotten the little knitted Superman doll stuffed into his jacket pocket. Sister was pleased to see a jolly face that she recognized and greeted him fondly saying, "I think little Johnny is in need of your cheery face, Alf." She pointed towards a corner of the ward where a painfully thin eight-year-old boy laid quietly in a spinal cast, suffering from severe scoliosis, "curvature of the spine," remarked Sister. Johnny had been in the hospital for several months already, he wasn't a happy child; he missed his family terribly, hated living in a cast, confined to his bed and was always so frightened. Loud noises particularly startled him and he cried very easily.

Alf tried as hard as he could to cheer the little boy up. It didn't seem appropriate at all to mention what a wonderful time he had just spent on the Margate sands, building castles, splashing in the sea and licking ice cream with a Cadbury's Flake. Alf's stash of chocolates when offered didn't help either. Then when Alf was beginning to give up Johnny suddenly asked, "What's that stuffed in your pocket?" A head was poking out and Alf remembered the superhero doll. For the first time that summer's afternoon Alf saw a spark of light in the little boy's sunken eyes. Johnny carefully examined the knitted toy, smiled and gently placed him on his chest, closed his eyes and said, "Alf, will you please tell me a story."

This was the beginning of a new chapter in their lives, Alf, the storyteller, and Johnny, the little waif, who in his dreams became a superhero. Alf had never considered himself a real storyteller but the simplicity of his stories peppered with some display of his physical prowess captured Johnny's imagination and the attention of the other young patients in adjoining beds. By the time the visiting bell rang Johnny's face had lit up, his cheeks were rosy and his eyes shone brightly almost as if he had been on an adventure himself free from the confines of his spinal cast and his hospital bed. Alf promised to return soon and left the faded Superman knitted doll with Johnny for safekeeping.

Alf returned to London that evening with the other cabbies and his happy brood, he had a pleasant glow in his heart. He had taken special needs children to Margate sands and a very needy young boy to a land of very special adventures. Alf smiled and sighed; today he knew that he had made a difference.

Ada wondered what had got into Alf .The couple had never managed to have any children of their own but currently her husband of thirty years had taken to ordering Superman comics at the corner newsagents shop and reading them while he was waiting for fares!

Alf never broke a promise, he was always true to his word and three weeks later he announced to Ada, "We are going to Margate for the day, please pack up a picnic ready for early tomorrow morning." This was the first of many visits that grew in frequency and regularity. Alf's day was mainly spent with Johnny and his superhero doll, and Ada liked to walk along the prom, taking in the clean sea air, and browsing the shops in Margate High Street. Alf's stories took Johnny to far off places, tales of adventures and heroism, tales of strength and endurance, tales of good versus bad. Johnny lived vicariously in his imagination; he became the superhero and in doing so his sickly body began to mend.

Johnny, the boys in adjoining beds and the nursing staff all called their regular visitor, "Grandpa Alf." Everyday when Alf had a day off he would exclaim to Ada, "Margate's calling!" They would pack a picnic and drive down for the day. Sister would always thank Alf for making such a difference. Johnny's improvement was almost miraculous; his doctors were so pleased with his progress that they speculated he would be able to return home many months earlier than expected. The love and dedication of a kind man and a superhero had healed a very sick little boy. Johnny had grown in strength and his severe spinal curvature greatly diminished. He continued to keep in touch with Alf and Ada, his Superman knitted doll took pride of place in his bedroom and when

Johnny eventually married the doll remained in his bedroom and continued to entertain his own children as they were growing up.

Alf always pondered where the knitted doll had come from that fateful day back in 1972; he also realized that good health and healing meant paying attention to your outlook in life. He began to wonder if unseen forces were guiding and enriching the lives of people everywhere. "Magic!" He exclaimed to Ada one day when they were quite old and browsing through their Margate photograph album. "Ada, Margate is a magical place, anything is possible when you have love and dedication!"

Poppy opened her eyes and looked down at the faded but still jaunty superhero. She smiled and fondly thought about Alf, Ada and little Johnny who had gained his strength and wellness through his dreams and imagination. She hugged the knitted doll, felt its magic and knew that she had another treasure.

Poppy set the box of Christmas ornaments and her magical doll on the wooden counter top and waited for Madam to come to the shop. Today she was late but this was just as well, a quiet, empty shop had afforded Poppy her own adventure back in time. Madam was delighted with the retro ornaments and dispatched Poppy in search of a Christmas tree. One of the greengrocers at the top of Margate High Street had just received a large shipment of cut fir trees of every shape and size. Poppy chose a modest tree just big enough to grace one of Madam's windows. The fresh intoxicating scent of pine needles made the haul back down the High Street an easier task. A hint of snow still remained in the air as the clouds continued to hang heavily across the harbour.

Margate Clock Tower struck two o'clock as Poppy and Madam were finishing up and admiring the tree now standing in the window. Retro ornaments and baubles beautified the fronds and Poppy quickly scribbled, "fairy lights" on her to-do list. Poppy suddenly remembered the knitted Superman doll and asked if he might grace the top of the tree. Madam Popoff looked thoughtfully at Poppy as she exclaimed, "Poppy dear, angels usually have pride of place on Christmas trees!" Poppy handed Madam the faded doll and simply replied, "But Madam this is an angel."

Madam's all seeing eyes and all knowing fingers lifted him gently from the oak counter and after a few minutes she smiled and simply said, "Yes, so he is. Well-done Poppy!"

Chapter 12

Poppy loved Christmas; she particularly loved the fairy lights and sparkling ornaments. She had been busy in the shop carefully sorting through party attire in the Madam Popoff Vintage Emporium and had arranged everything on the dressmaker dummies or the clothing rack nearest the shop door. As she busied herself she once again looked wistfully up at the exquisite bag with the beaded irises blowing in the wind. No one had purchased it. "Waiting," muttered Poppy to herself as she pondered the bag's future journey in time.

"Waiting!" Exclaimed Poppy to Jack the Lad as she cycled along the windy promenade at Westbrook. She stopped just before the Royal Sea Bathing Hospital building. The hospital had closed many years ago and now the old building had been converted into luxury apartments. Hospital days were over but since the appearance of the knitted Superman doll she had wondered what other stories the old walls could tell. Today what had really caught Poppy's eye was an old terraced house overlooking the sea adjacent to the former hospital. The windows were painted a bright yellow and a lovely Christmas tree with golden baubles graced the main front room window but like the Superman doll this too was faded and had belonged to another time. Poppy surveyed all the other windows and these too were decorated for the season. It was such a strange house, Poppy first noticed it several years ago on her annual visits to Aunt Flora and here it was still completely unchanged. Time appeared to stand still in this house, and it remained forever Christmas.

"Waiting," Poppy whispered again. The cold air still felt like snow and Jack the Lad was wrapped up in a bright woollen jacket carefully knitted by Isadora's sister. He had cocked his head and had been watching Poppy intently. He was waiting for her to turn the bike around and head in the direction of Ramsgate. Winston and the fat sausages would be waiting for him there. At long last Poppy obliged and off they ventured to Ship Shape Café.

Once Poppy and Jack the Lad were warmly situated inside she began to ponder over the Christmas house. Margate certainly had its fair share of unusual places but Christmas forever particularly captured her attention. "How curious, is someone stuck in the past, unable to move on from loss and grief?' She asked Jack the Lad and Winston. The two little dogs, bellies full with sausage, were happy to sit and listen to Poppy's musings as she continued, "Perhaps they just really love Christmas. It brings such happy memories usually of childhood when the magic of the bright lights, Father Christmas and the expectation of new toys prevail." The little dogs, heads cocked to one side, continued to quietly listen. Poppy then chided herself, "Madam Popoff told me not to speculate, I learnt that lesson with the lovely linen tea cloths embroidered by Dennis."

Poppy sighed, she was learning a lot about life since she had moved to Margate but she resigned herself to the fact that unlike Madam, she just didn't know or understand everything.

Poppy pedalled Dora much faster in the colder weather; so the ride from Ramsgate Harbour to The Market Place in Margate currently took half the time. Jack the Lad was extremely relieved to return to the warmth of Lookout Retreat, as he was cold and windswept. He barked as Poppy mounted her bicycle again, waved him goodbye, and set off towards the town.

It was two weeks before Christmas, the beautifully decorated freshly cut fir tree in the window delighted passers by. Business had become brisk. Madam asked Isadora to move a couple of the Singer sewing tables onto the shop floor. The lovely linen tea cloths carefully made by Dennis graced the tables and Madam set out plates of warm sweet mincemeat pies, mugs and a little urn kept filled with hot apple cider. The smell of warm sweet mince pies drew in even more shoppers A small tin and a lifeboat collecting box were set out too with a note asking for donations to "The Salvation Army Christmas Appeal and The Royal National Lifeboat Institution."

As Margate Clock Tower struck three o'clock a lively group of teenage girls crossed the threshold. They giggled and chatted as they rifled through the racks of vintage clothing and the shelves of other paraphernalia. One of the girls looked slightly older, perhaps in her early twenties. She appeared much more grown up but still carried the youthful exuberance of the others. She was looking for an evening bag to complement her beautiful blue and gold silk dress interestingly adorned with an iris design. She had purchased the dress several months ago in the end of summer sales out at The Westwood Cross Shopping Centre.

According to Poppy's observation she had noticed the exquisite bag with beaded irises blowing in the wind at the same time that she had seen the lifeboat collecting box sitting nearby on the Singer sewing machine table set with mince pies and hot apple cider. "Oh!" She exclaimed, "I'm so happy to see that you have a lifeboat collecting box. I'm a Parker girl, you know! My family has been connected to the Margate Lifeboat forever! Actually, I'm set to attend the lifeboat dinner and dance this weekend and I've been searching for a bag to match my new party dress."

Madam Popoff, roly-poly and her face wizened with age, appeared from behind the large costume mirror. Smiling broadly she took her hand and said, "Yes dear, we've been waiting for you to come in and this bag has been patiently waiting for you too." When Madam placed the exquisite bag in her hands everyone knew that the perfect match had been made. "Magic!" Exclaimed the lively group of girls in unison. As the Parker girl gently caressed the beautiful beaded iris design and drew it close to her heart she really knew that this bag was truly meant for her. *Those weavers of everything unseen* had crafted her name on it.

"Waiting for the right time," Poppy muttered to her herself, and so it was that the exquisite bag with the beaded iris design blowing in the wind was ready to begin a new journey of belonging. Madam, Poppy and Isadora waved to the jolly band of teenagers and to the Parker girl as they crossed the threshold. There was joy in all of their hearts, "It is going to be a great Christmas!" Exclaimed Poppy.

Chapter 13

The following day Poppy made an impulsive visit to The Margate Lifeboat House before opening up the shop. Her curious nature had spurred her onto finding out more, specifically about the Parker family who now had ownership of the clutch bag. The Lifeboat House was open for visitors and Poppy climbed the steps to reach the upper level where some memorabilia was displayed. There she found a wonderful framed tribute to Coxswain Edward Duke Parker who was awarded, *The Distinguished Service Medal*, for the evacuation of 600 troops from the beaches of Dunkirk. Also on display was the house flag of, *The Association of the Little Ships of Dunkirk.* This flag was displayed along with Ted Parker's photograph, his medal and a plaque celebrating his crew. Poppy noted that two other Parkers' were on the lifeboat, *The Lord Southborough Civil Service No 1* during the evacuation.

Poppy continued her cycle ride to Marine Gardens down by Margate Clock Tower where there was a board celebrating the 150th anniversary of Margate's Lifeboat. Part of the inscription read as follows:

--- *The commanding officer of the destroyer HMS Icarus stated "The manner in which the Margate Lifeboat crew brought off load after load of soldiers under continuous shelling, bombing and aerial machine gun fire, will be an inspiration to us all as long as we live." Edward Duke Parker was awarded the DSM for his leadership but he attributed it to the whole crew.*

Poppy sighed, she fully realized that the exquisite bag with the beaded irises blowing in the wind never had her name on it, but it had found a good home with the Parker family. She recalled Madam Popoff's words:

"Sometimes in life Poppy, there are things that we want, things that we can well afford to buy, things that we fall in love with, but actually they don't belong to us and we don't deserve them. More to the point, Poppy, they won't be happy with us!" Poppy smiled, deep in her heart she knew that the bag would be happy with the Parker girl, after all they really did share history, the silver thread that connects people, places, events and time.

Madam Popoff Vintage Emporium had been busier than ever the two weeks leading up to Christmas. The Tuesday and Friday morning soirees were particularly successful. Ollie played carols on his heavenly harp and Poppy, Aunt Flora and Isadora had baked some rich Christmas fruitcakes and decorated them with royal icing. The regular customers brought in friends and neighbours and Madam had to send Poppy out to neighbouring shops to see if they could borrow some extra chairs. Sizable sums of money were collected for local charities including The RNLI and The Salvation Army Christmas Appeal Fund. Extra people meant more browsers in the shop and a surprising number of people bought some thing. Madam had an eclectic mix of sparkly costume jewellery in a glass display case and this provided a number of Christmas gifts for the happy shoppers.

Madam decided to close early on Christmas Eve and not to re open until well into the New Year. "We are all really tired and in need of a holiday," she announced the week before Christmas. Christmas Eve was quieter; most people had finished their gift shopping. Isadora wasn't coming in, she was busy helping her sister plan for a children's party in the afternoon.

Margate Clock Tower struck one o'clock and Poppy was looking forward to the two o' clock closing and the prospect of a nice long break. It was cold and windy outside but still there was no snow. The Christmas tree, adorned with fairy lights and retro ornaments, lit up the window with a comforting glow and on top of it all presided the kitted Superman, faded but still jaunty.

The shop door suddenly opened and a young mother pushing a large buggy made for a disabled boy attempted to manoeuvre her way over the threshold. Poppy ran to her aid and beamed. The boy looked about five years old but his mother had already read Poppy's mind and said, "Hello this is Angus and he's eight years old. He's not very well, he has something wrong with the bones in his back and he has to wear a special brace. It's called scoliosis." Poppy smiled, "please do come in and have a warm mince pie."

Angus really did look sickly, his eyes were sunken, his arms and legs were painfully thin and he looked fed up. Poppy smiled and addressed Angus, "what are you hoping that Father Christmas will bring you tomorrow, Angus?" He didn't answer but simply turned his head away; bit his lips and Poppy could see tears welling up in his eyes.

Madam had been watching and listening from behind the large costume mirror and beckoned to Poppy to come over. When they were both out of hearing distance Madam instructed Poppy to quietly remove the Superman angel whilst she kept the family otherwise occupied. "Please take it to the back room, find an old box and wrap it with some of the Christmas wrapping paper stored in the dresser." Poppy gently removed the superhero from the top of the tree, kissed him goodbye and lovingly packed him up. As she did so she asked the jaunty little toy to take good care of Angus and to weave his healing magic.

Angus sat in the buggy looking quite glum while his mother browsed the sparkly costume jewellery in the glass cabinet. She made a small purchase and readied to leave. Madam took her aside, squeezed her hand and told her that the Madam Popoff Vintage Emporium had a very special gift for Angus. Madam slipped the nicely wrapped gift into a large Tesco bag so that Angus wouldn't see the Christmas wrapping. "Happy Christmas my dears I think it will be a good one," she whispered.

The Christmas tree certainly looked different, the angel had gone. Madam sensed Poppy's concern, "Poppy dear, we all have to learn to let things go, wave them on with joy in our hearts. Angus needs that toy more than our shop window. The unseen forces drew them here today; it was the right time for Angus. Christmas will be over and gone quite soon, Angus's suffering won't be so quick but a jaunty little superhero may just make the passage of time needed to heal his suffering mind and body shorter and more manageable."

They hugged each other, turned off all the lights, except the fairy ones on the Christmas tree, and buttoned up their coats as they trod very carefully over the threshold and into the crisp Margate air.

As it was only two o'clock Poppy wasn't quite ready to return to Lookout Retreat. The sun was shining brightly in a sky of sparkling blue. Poppy decided to cycle along the Margate seafront promenade towards The Royal Sea Bathing Hospital building. She still had Angus on her mind and she had begun to recall little Johnny, Alf and Ada from all those years ago. She cycled past the lone lifeboat man gazing out to the Nayland Rock. This is the memorial dedicated to the memory of the men who drowned through the overturning of The Margate Surf Life Boat, *Friend To All Nations*, in the great storm of December 2nd, 1897.

Shortly after passing the memorial Poppy stopped her bicycle on the promenade and looked at the forever Christmas house. Time stood still here, "waiting," muttered Poppy to herself. As she continued to ponder a roly-poly old lady appeared seemingly out of nowhere. Poppy had never actually seen Madam Popoff out of her shop before and Madam had never referred to her home. There had only ever been one reference to a place other than the Madam Popoff Vintage Emporium and that was when Madam talked about taking undesirable things to her allotment garden and burning them.

In truth, Madam remained a mystery. "Poppy, dear it's best not to linger here, sometimes it's not for us to ask questions and it's not for us to receive answers either. Some things are best left alone. Don't meddle." Poppy turned her head away to gaze at the forever Christmas tree adorned with faded golden baubles and when she looked back towards Madam she had disappeared. There was such a lot that Poppy didn't understand. However, she had definitely been learning lessons in *The Madam Popoff Wisdom School* since she had started her new job. Just like the jaunty superhero doll, Madam remained an enigma.

59

Poppy continued her cycle ride along the promenade and paused again by The Royal Sea Bathing Hospital building. Time certainly hadn't stopped still here; there had been many changes. The old hospital and its patients were gone, replaced by expensive, luxury flats constructed within the heart of the old building. However, the hospital chapel still remained in tact. Poppy recalled reading the history of the chapel; apparently during the evacuation of Dunkirk it had been used as an extra hospital ward. An unconscious soldier had woken up in the chapel, looked around at the beautiful stained glass windows and declared to his neighbouring bedfellow that they were all in heaven now!

"Heaven!" Poppy shouted out to the clear blue sky and the shining sea as she began to turn many things over in her mind. "There's Ollie and his heavenly harp, Madam Popoff who seems to know everything and who's so charitable and then there's Margate and its special people. There are the men from the Margate Surfboat, *Friend To All Nations,* and the Margate men who risked their own lives to bring the troops home from Dunkirk. There's Ted Parker and *The Lord Southborough* and Iris the angelic nurse. There's Lily who wouldn't let Dennis go and nursed him in a garden shed for the best part of two years, then there's Alf and Ada whose love and a superhero doll made a huge difference to a very sick boy."

Poppy closed her eyes, took a deep breath and thanked Margate and its people for their loving embrace and for making a difference in her life. As she did so she heard the sweet music of Christmas carols coming from deep within the Royal Sea Bathing Hospital building, drifting out over the Westbrook Bay.

"Carols, Poppy dear!" Exclaimed Aunt Flora. Poppy was sitting by a blazing fire back at Lookout Retreat with Jack the Lad curled up on her lap. They had just finished a delicious Christmas Eve supper. Aunt Flora continued to reminisce, "Years ago I volunteered with The Royal Sea Bathing Hospital League of Friends. I was a lot younger then. Bertie and I would join the others and we would all sing carols in the wards on

Christmas Eve. The patients loved it, the dedicated staff had gone to great lengths to decorate the hospital and provide lots of seasonal goodies to make up for the fact that they were away from the comfort of their own home at Christmas time. Walls have memories Poppy; it was the friends who came to sing every Christmas. That's what you heard today." Poppy was so glad that she had sold her home in London, given up her PR job and moved to Margate. She felt the warmth of love and friendship here and was no longer lonely.

It was very late; Aunt Flora and the dogs were tucked up in bed as Poppy stepped out of Lookout Retreat. The sky was inky black, the stars shone brightly and the moon lit up the streets. Poppy drew her scarf more tightly around her neck and pulled her woollen beret down over her ears as she hurried along to the midnight service at St Paul's Church, Cliftonville. The air was still crisp and there was the possibility of snow.

The church was aglow with hundreds of little tea lights; it was quite magical as she stepped inside to a warm welcome. As Poppy sat throughout the service and the congregation sang, *Oh, little town of Bethlehem*, she thought of all that had transpired since she had taken the last train to Margate back in the summer. She considered how much she had grown in confidence and how much she had learnt about being human. She looked down at her long, delicate fingers she was learning to feel her way through life and to realize that true healing begins with one's outlook in life. She had begun to acknowledge that where there is love there's often grief, as people have to say goodbye and let go of their loved ones. Where there is anger there must be room for understanding and forgiveness and where there is fear there must be room for courage. She especially thought about Ted Parker and the crew of *The Lord Southborough,* men who risked their own lives to save those who were strangers. As the clock struck midnight and heralded Christmas morning she said a prayer for all those connected with the little town of Margate, those from the past, for those she knew now and for those who would witness a time that she would never see.

Chapter 14

The New Year brought much colder weather but at least the sky was a beautiful clear blue and the sun was shining. Poppy was sitting sipping a cup of coffee within the warm confines of Ship Shape Café. She could hear the gulls wheeling outside the partly open door but it was far too cold to sit outside. The café, situated under the arches on Ramsgate harbour, was busy with lots of the regular customers ordering fully cooked English breakfasts. There was the comforting smell of bacon, sausages and eggs and as Poppy looked around she muttered to herself, "this is such a cheery, homely place." Lobster pots and nets hung from the white washed barrel ceiling and a number of model ships and lanterns sat on the shelves around the cavernous interior. An RNLI collecting box sat on the counter top near the till. Poppy looked down at the two happy dogs sitting under her table.

Mary had taken a New Year bargain break holiday to Spain in search of some warmer weather and Aunt Flora had graciously offered to "room" Winston at Lookout Retreat during her absence. Mary had been quite concerned because Winston, being a dog of routine, wouldn't be settled unless he received his daily sausage from Ship Shape Café. Aunt Flora promised to cook him a sausage for his breakfast every day but Mary said that simply wouldn't do, it had to be a Ship Shape sausage! Poppy was worried; she knew that she couldn't fit two Jack Russell terriers into her bicycle basket. Aunt Flora, after a lot of thought, suddenly had her eureka moment! "Poppy dear, call next door and ask the good people at Seaside Villa if you can borrow their bicycle chariot, that contraption that they tow behind when they take their two toddlers out for a spin."

So early every morning two little dogs sat majestically in their chariot whilst Poppy pedalled with more gusto than usual to reach Ship Shape Café and the sausages. Poppy smiled as she continued to look down at the two contented dogs under her feet, she began to consider the New Year, what adventures and new insights the Madam Popoff Vintage Emporium might bring.

As Poppy was readying herself to return to work within the next few days she decided to have one last fling with the chariot and take the dogs down to Marine Sands to watch the blessing of the sea. This is a colourful religious ceremony held each January since 1964 to mark the Feast of Epiphany. Margate has a large Greek Cypriot community and the town was selected for this honour in the mid 1960's. The celebration begins with a service at St Michael the Archangel, the Greek Orthodox Church in Margate, followed by a procession of clergy and local dignitaries parading down to the sea. Doves are released, prayers given and a decorated cross is hurled into the sea to be retrieved by young divers for the Greek Orthodox Archbishop. It was cold but the bright red coats of the dignitaries, the clergy dressed in their finery and the pipes, drums, trumpets and whistles of the marching band warmed Poppy's heart. She positioned herself by the Surfboat Memorial. Poppy was also in close proximity to the forever Christmas house. The New Year Blessing of the sea reminded her of all that had happened since taking the last train to Margate and the seaside, it was only last summer but it seemed like an eternity.

Chapter 15

Poppy, Madam and Isadora were all refreshed after the long Christmas break and the New Year brought new ideas too. Madam decided to put a note in the window asking for old fashion magazines, books and journals along with vintage dressmaking patterns. "Anything before 1980 will do," she declared "the older the better, we are a costume emporium and anything associated with the world of fashion will be welcome here, this will add extra interest."

Poppy was excited about the prospect of old dressmaking patterns. She had observed the growing interest in dresses from the 1940 – 1960's and knew that not everyone wanted the old clothes. They wanted, the look, but clothes made with fresh fabric. Growing numbers of young people were becoming interested in learning how to sew and there was definitely a market for fashionable designs from another era but made from bright new fabrics.

A few days later Poppy arrived early one morning and found a pile of literature carefully bundled up with brown string and left propped up on the doorstep. Once she had finished her general tidy up and settled down with a cup of coffee she realized that the bundle had arrived in response to Madam's recent note in the shop window asking for vintage fashion journals and dressmaking patterns. There were lots of Vogue and Simplicity patterns and some old Vogue magazines. Poppy was just contemplating where and how they might be displayed when a thin tattered booklet fell to the floor. It was, *"The Twelve Healers,"* by Edward Bach printed in Epsom 1933. Poppy picked it up and set it aside on the oak countertop where it lay alone and quite forgotten until Poppy was ready to give it her attention.

Valentine's Day was on everyone's mind and Isadora was spearheading a massive decorating campaign to entice more customers to call into the shop. Poppy was given the task of sorting through everything in stock that was either red or had a love theme. There were red costumes, red shoes, red bags, red gloves and red hats all needing to be artistically displayed throughout the shop. Ball gowns vied for position in Madam's large picture windows facing onto King Street. Madam was also planning a Valentine's afternoon charity tea party for the lonely elderly and this would happen on the two afternoons before Valentine's Day and on the day itself. Madam's Tuesday and Friday morning soirees had been a tremendous success and she currently received many requests for other events during the long cold winter weather. People loved Ollie's heavenly harp and he suggested that he brought along his pal Cedric who played the violin. Aunt Flora had been thrilled to hear about the tea party arrangements and was looking forward to baking trays of Valentine heart shape biscuits, fairy cakes with pink icing and preparing Spanish strawberries, dipped in dark chocolate. Of course she was also preparing to read the tealeaves.

A few days later Poppy was on her own busy sorting through piles of clothing in the back room. The shop was locked up; opening time wasn't until 11am so she had a few hours to get on top of the Valentine situation. Valentine's Day was never a good time of the year for Poppy, she had experienced so many disappointments and failed relationships in the past and now when it came to affairs of the heart she would rather pass. She lacked both the courage and the inclination to dip her toes into the vast ocean of emotional uncertainty. Fear of yet another failure kept the men away and Poppy on the shelf. The word "waiting" once more came to mind. Poppy was never sure exactly what she was waiting for but many of her friends had often mentioned the word "courage!"

The early 1950's ball dress was beautiful; it had arrived the previous day in a cardboard box left on the doorstep with a number of other odds and ends. There were layers of white chiffon and net petticoats with tiny yellow flowers embroidered on the bodice and on the overskirt. Poppy could imagine the dress on the mannequin in Madam's picture window along with the lovely red slippers and the matching evening bag that she had sorted through. She visualized a red rose in the mannequin's hair.

"Perfect!" Poppy exclaimed, "This will be a crowd stopper." She set to work and an hour later made herself a cup of coffee and settled down to look at the fruit of her efforts. The mannequin was dressed and ready to be placed in the shop window. Poppy gently touched the frothy white chiffon decorated with the tiny yellow flowers, she shut her eyes and once again she was transported back to, another time.

It was Valentine's Day 1953 and Edna looked absolutely stunning. A wealthy friend from London had given her the ball gown for her birthday back in early January. She was quite lost in a sea of billowing white foam and tiny yellow flowers. Bill, her dashing American airman had invited her to the Manston Airfield dance to be held at The Dreamland Ballroom that evening. A Big Band would be playing. Edna was excited; she had been stepping out with her airman for the best part of ten weeks, in fact since shortly after he joined the base at Manston. During The Cold War of the 1950's the US Air Force used RAF Manston as a strategic Air Command Base for its bomber and fighter-bomber units. They met in the Joe Lyons teashop in Margate High Street. Edna had been having tea with a teaching colleague and she slipped on the icy step as she was leaving. Bill came to her rescue and they became inseparable since that fateful day. Sadly Edna's mother wasn't having any of it.

Edna was a shy young lady, she was nervous, lots of things worried her and to top it all she was painfully indecisive. Her domineering mother worried her the most. Mother continually warned her that men were nothing but trouble; they arrived, did some wooing and eventually left you to pick up the broken pieces. Edna's mother was particularly bitter and angry; her own husband had left her with a young baby and a string of debt as he sailed away into the sunset and into the arms of another woman. She had been left to raise her child alone, the divorce, very unusual for all those years ago, had been very nasty and both Edna and her mother had come off badly.

Edna's mother was possessive after all Edna was all that she had left she certainly wasn't going to let her daughter go into the arms of some Yank at the airbase. Edna didn't do too much to help herself, she was afraid of her mother and gave her a wide berth when ever she had the chance but she could never bring herself to leave the family home and stand on her own two feet. Edna could well have afforded to set herself up with her own place. At 25 years old most of her friends and colleagues were already married and many had families of their own. Edna had graduated from teacher training college, and held down a nice cosy job teaching at a Margate Infants School. Despite her nervous, timid disposition, she was popular with the children and her colleagues. Bill called her his, "sweetheart."

Two girlfriends called for Edna on Valentine's evening, planning to share a cab to Dreamland and to meet up with their airmen companions. Edna's mother, always ready to make life difficult watched as Edna glided down the stairs in her ball gown. Sadly she offered no encouraging comments or pleasantries, just a few inappropriate remarks about men in general, which left a bitter taste in everyone's mouth.

The dance was wonderful everyone was so happy. Edna felt really special in her stunning ball gown with her red shoes and the red ribbon tying back her long blonde hair. It was a night when all the young people could kick back and forget the austerity of the post war years. Bill had been stationed at nearby Hawkinge Airfield in Kent during the Second World War and had lost many of his fellow pilots in the dogfights that took place over the South Coast. They had all been so young back in the 1940's and all so fearful when they had left the air base on sorties. No one knew who would return and who would never come back. Bill was familiar with uncertainty and it was in this spirit of uncertainty that Bill decided he would ask for Edna's hand in marriage. On his day off he had gone into Margate and visited S.H. Cuttings the Margate jeweller. He chose a lovely ruby ring. Bill was 33 years old now and an officer, deployment at Manston Airfield usually lasted 90 days and it was very likely that he and his unit would be moved on very soon. There was talk of them heading to Japan for combat duty in the Korean War. He had grown to love Edna, albeit in such a short time, but if he waited he knew that he might lose her.

Edna hadn't anticipated Bill's proposal at all it hit her like a brick falling from above, painful and unexpected. She muttered to herself, "What would mother say? Could I ever leave mother and move to America?" The stress of it all brought on a sudden migraine and an early exit from the ballroom. Edna told Bill that she needed time to think about things she had pushed the ring away and asked for a cab home. Bill was broken hearted; he had anticipated champagne, a hasty wedding before deployment and a future with a sweetheart who would wait for him to return. There was nothing sweet about Bill's return to the air base that night.

Bill still had Edna's photograph and the ruby ring from S.H. Cuttings in his flying suit breast pocket when his Lockheed F-94 Starfire interceptor plunged into the Pacific Ocean. Edna eventually received a letter from one of Bill's closest friends informing her that he had been killed in action.

Over the years that followed Edna lost herself in her work and taking care of her aging mother. When her own retirement loomed she found herself alone in the small home that she had once shared with her mother, she never married she had no children of her own and there had been no more balls to attend. Of course she had plenty of friends, her teaching colleagues and the ladies from the WI but the house was empty and there was a deep wound that lingered in her heart. Edna couldn't alter the clock, she could never go back and rewrite history she couldn't fix what had happened that Valentine's night but sadly she hadn't been able to venture forward either. Edna some how remained frozen on Valentine's Day in 1953. Frozen in her own indecision and fears and the frothy white ball gown with the tiny yellow flowers remained frozen too. It was locked away in a large trunk, stored in the attic and quite forgotten until the young family who purchased the home after Edna's death started renovations.

Poppy was crying when Madam made an appearance. She looked at Poppy, then at the beautifully dressed mannequin and simply said, "To dress and mend the broken pieces, that's what we do here, Poppy. This dress has a lot of history and just look at those beautiful yellow flowers they are called *Mimulus*."

Poppy thought it odd that Madam had drawn her attention to the tiny yellow flowers and that she mentioned their specific name. She had never heard this name before but she filed it away in her growing book of wisdom. She got up and made a cup of coffee for them both before gently lifting the mannequin into the window. Isadora had picked up strings of heart shaped fairy lights from the DIY store and this kept them both busy for the rest of the morning.

Chapter 16

"Silently, one by one, in the infinite meadows of heaven, blossomed the lovely stars, the forget –me –knots of the angels."

Springtime had arrived in Margate. The gardens and parks were covered with golden daffodils and primroses; the colour yellow seemed to be everywhere. It reminded Poppy of the tiny yellow *Mimulus* flowers on Edna's frothy white dress. The Valentine window was history now and the dress had been carefully hung up in the evening gown section of Madam's vintage emporium still waiting for new ownership. The old tattered booklet, *"The Twelve Healers,"* by Edward Bach sat unopened and gathering dust on the oak countertop.

The days were becoming warmer and Poppy was beginning to enjoy her early morning bike rides, less of an effort without the icy wind biting at her as she pedalled. Poppy loved the ride around the coast particularly between Cliftonville and Broadstairs and up near the North Foreland Lighthouse at Kingsgate there was a field full of donkeys that she liked to visit. A notice had recently appeared on the fence:

"Please give the animals only carrots and apples. Thank you."

Jack the Lad couldn't read but he knew that the note must be very important since Poppy spent such a long time looking at it. In truth, it had jogged her memory. Last week a small box had arrived on Madam's doorstep filled with odds and ends, mainly sparkly costume jewellery but amongst the sparkles there was a tiny, rather unusual treasure. It was a little vintage brooch, a donkey fashioned out of gold with a tiny seed pearl for an eye. Poppy decided that she needed to find out more about its story; it seemed to be calling her. Jack the Lad was becoming impatient; sausages and Winston were calling for him!

Later that day, when Poppy was alone in the shop, she sat down and carefully examined the little brooch and as her long delicate fingers moved across the little animal she was taken back to another time.

Ted was late in fact he was always late. He heard Margate Clock Tower as it struck 10 o'clock; he should have had the donkeys on the beach nearly 30 minutes ago. It was 1909, Edwardian Margate, and a very busy summer for the town. The hotels and boarding houses were full of visitors, and business was particularly good. The sun had shone throughout most of July and now it was early August and it was even hotter. The paddle steam ships were coming down from London on a regular schedule and dropping off the holidaymakers at the end of the Margate Jetty. Today *The Golden Eagle* was tied up. Deck chair attendants were beginning to set up the chairs on Marine Sands and the horses were already harnessed to the bathing machines as they waited in a long line on the sands to take bathers into the water.

Ted was a donkey boy. He was 14 years old and lived with his large family in the old town just off King Street. Life was hard; the tiny family home was crowded, money was always tight and Ted's father was mean and often drunk. He would rant and rave and thrash Ted with his belt. Ted was a sensitive soul, who loved animals and always seemed to be daydreaming. In his mind he would go to other places, far away from his violent father and the squalor and chaos of the family home. Ted couldn't seem to learn in school, his mind was always somewhere else. When he left he could barely read and write but he was very good with animals.

Ted loved the donkeys; he knew all their names and their idiosyncrasies. He talked to them late at night when he should have been home. He would stay on at the stables, sit on a bale of hay and tell them stories of far off places, knights and castles, people who lived in nice homes with nice parents who did fun things. The homes were warm, there were comfortable beds and there was always food on the dining table. In fact the donkey stables near St John's Church were Ted's comfortable place and this is where he would dream.

When Ted did put in an appearance at home his mother would scream and tell him to get his feet on the ground and help clear up the mess. The house was always a mess, too many bodies sharing a confined space, bed bugs and cockroaches, father's beer bottles and damp mould growing up the walls because Margate Old Town was prone to flooding. In contrast the stables were dry and clean; the donkeys were always well looked after by the donkey boys, who brought in the money. Donkeys on Margate beach made the iconic photograph along with the lines of bathing machines. Margate was the first seaside resort to feature donkey rides on the sands in 1890, and the first resort to introduce deck chairs back in 1898.

That day in early August 1909 stayed in Ted's mind for the rest of his life. Sid and Jack were helping him lead the train of donkeys, Ted was in front leading Dolly, Jack was in the middle and Sid took up the rear with Jasper. They had slowly snaked down Margate High Street and were just about to turn left and go down Elephant Hill towards Margate Clock Tower and the sands when it happened. It was a terrible accident.

There were very few motorcars on the road and those who owned or drove them were extremely wealthy. Mabel and her young son, John, were staying as guests with John Lubbock, The Lord Avebury up at Kingsgate Castle. Lord Avebury's chauffeur was in the driving seat; Mabel and John sat on the back seat of The Rolls Royce Silver Ghost. They had passed through Cecil Square and were at the top of Elephant Hill. Ted saw it first, he was holding Dolly's leading rein when a stray dog ran across the road in hot pursuit of a feral cat. The car braked so suddenly that it lost control, skidded across the road, hit a steep step and overturned.

In the commotion that followed Ted clearly heard an urgent voice he could have sworn that Dolly was talking to him, "Get them out right now don't wait, hurry, there's not much time!" Ted whistled to Jack and Sid to come running, shopkeepers spilled onto the street and Ted called for them to hold onto the donkeys. Sid and Jack were burly boys, better built and much stronger than Ted, but all three boys helped. Once again he heard Dolly's urgent voice calling to him, "Hurry Ted, there's not much time."

It took all Ted's energy and strength to drag the lady and her boy out first and then the boys went back for the chauffeur. As soon as they were done Ted heard Dolly's voice again, "Hurry, get everyone to run Ted, run, run now." Ted didn't remember much, he knew he had shouted to everyone and he recalled running when suddenly the car caught fire.

The papers called it, *The Miracle on Elephant Hill.* Yes, it was a miracle that Mabel, John and the chauffeur came out of it all relatively unscathed and no onlookers were injured. They had heard Ted's urgent voice commanding them to run on that fateful day. The donkeys curiously had remained silent and orderly throughout the whole episode with just the occasional bray from Dolly. Lord Avebury, in his gratitude, had S.H. Cutting the jeweller and goldsmith in Margate Old Town make three little donkey brooches for the fine young donkey boys who had lent a helping hand that day and gallantly saved three lives.

Up at the stables Ted became known as the "Donkey Whisperer" the boys all made fun of him but deep down they all knew that Ted was special. He possessed a gift that seemed to set him apart from the other lads; everyone could see how much he loved his donkeys and how much they loved him too. He wore his little gold donkey brooch with pride but never took it home, having a secret hiding place for it up at the stables. Ted knew that his father might take it away from him in a drunken fit and pawn it for extra beer money.

When the First World War broke out five years later during the summer of 1914 Ted, Sid and Jack dutifully signed up, taking the train to Canterbury to register for military service with the East Kent Regiment known as, *The Buffs.* Their experience with the donkeys was seen as a most important asset because horses and donkeys were used extensively to help transport supplies to the troops. One million horses, donkeys and mules were conscripted from the United Kingdom and used during the war but sadly only 62,000 returned after the conflict ended.

Ted and Jack eventually found themselves together again in northeastern France in 1917. They were so very war weary. It had gone on much longer than anyone had anticipated, and trench life was awful. The air vibrated with the tap and rattle of the Vickers machine gun fire, the whistle of bullets and there was always the threat of a gas attack along with the mud and stench of disease and death. Hostile aircraft overhead would sometimes drop bombs. The lads would keep slugs in a jar because they would visibly indicate their discomfort by closing their breathing pores and compressing their bodies. When they saw this happening the lads would quickly reach for their gas masks. They found bioluminescent allies in the glow worms and these also would be kept in jars. They would use their light to illuminate messages and maps in the darkness of the trenches.

Of course there was always the all-pervading fear of death and the anguish of losing a comrade. Ted loved his donkeys; he found solace in their company and mourned their loss as much as that of a close friend. Ted would sit with them and dream of other places far away from the filth and terror. Under his uniform shirt he wore his little gold donkey brooch and he came to look upon it as a talisman, something that would protect him and keep him from harm's way.

It was early September and Ted found himself in no man's land one night, he had gone out with the engineers to help mark a safe path for the next day when the troops had planned to go over the top and claim more ground in no man's land. That night something terrible happened. Their little group became lost; there was tremendous fear that the Germans might spot them and there was fear that if they didn't return by first light their own troops would shoot them. Ted, in his grave anxiety, rubbed his little donkey brooch and there it was again, Dolly's voice suddenly booming in his ear, "Stars Ted, look to the stars, they will guide you safely back."

The lads looked up to the heavens for help, Ted knew the constellations well. Farm boys had often worked at the donkey stables and they had taught Ted as he spent the long evenings with the donkeys in an effort to avoid the chaos of his own home. Of course Ted's favourite was the large and prominent northern constellation of Pegasus the white, winged horse of Greek mythology, used by Zeus to carry thunder and lightning from Mount Olympus. It was visible high in the sky starting near the end of the summer and continuing through the autumn and best seen during the months of September and October. Pegasus is a large pattern of stars marked by a great square, four bright stars form the body of the winged horse. Well, that particular night Dolly, the constellation of Pegasus together with Polaris, the North Star, guided four very anxious young men to safety. Ted never forgot the incident and privately thanked his own special angel, his little gold donkey brooch with the seed pearl eye.

One of Ted's comrades in the trenches, an educated young man, later recalled the words of the poet Henry Wadsworth Longfellow and shared them with the four lucky lads:

"Silently, one by one, in the infinite meadows of heaven, blossomed the lovely stars, the forget –me –knots of the angels."

Ted was one of the very lucky ones. At the end of the war he returned home to Margate. Things had dramatically changed; many of his brave young friends were either dead or had been left badly wounded, disabilities that they would carry to the end of their lives. Several suffered from shell shock and experienced tormenting nightmares every night. There had been damage to the town from the German zeppelins and planes but it was Ramsgate that had particularly suffered. The buildings bore the scars just as those who returned from the battlefields bore their own physical and emotional scars.

War was ugly, "Nothing good about it," Ted would tell those who had been left at home. Margate sands had been open for business throughout the war years; people had still holidayed and enjoyed all that the town had to offer despite the fact that so much death and destruction prevailed just a short distance over the horizon. Ted was war weary but nevertheless it had left him a resourceful man. His father had passed away; the doctors had called it "a bad liver." Now it fell upon Ted to help his mother and the younger ones who were still at home. Somehow the war had helped to place his two feet firmly on the ground, his dreaming days were over and he took an apprentice job with a kind electrician who needed extra help. Ted learnt a trade and eventually married a Margate girl but he never forgot his donkeys.

When the Second World War began Ted was older. He volunteered with the Home Guard. The shoreline was closed and barbed wire prevented people from stepping onto the sands. Ted was one of the many Margate men who helped the 49,342 soldiers ashore as the little ships and *The Lord Southborough* ferried them to the Margate Jetty during the crisis at Dunkirk.

Later in life, with more time on his hands, and when no one could find him they always remembered to look at the local stables. Ted would often sit on a bale of hay and tell the donkeys stories usually of Pegasus and the other constellations in the night sky. Sometimes he would reflect upon that night so many years ago, he would gently finger his little gold brooch and fondly think of Dolly, Lord Avebury and the grace that saved his life that night.

As Poppy opened her eyes, the little gold brooch with the seed pearl eye seemed to glow in her hand. She looked at her watch, it seemed as if hours had passed but it was just *a wrinkle in time*. She sighed, got up and went to find a nice gift box from the back room. Poppy lined it with a piece of red velvet and set the donkey brooch inside. The box sat on Poppy's special shelf, where the exquisite bag with the beaded irises blowing in the wind had patiently waited until the Parker girl had called by. Madam Popoff appeared from behind the large costume mirror, she smiled and nodded her head as she glided past the shelf; "time to go home Poppy, time to shut up the shop."

Chapter 17

Easter was on the horizon; Poppy and Isadora had put their heads together and decided to do something about the shop windows. Madam Popoff Vintage Emporium had an eclectic stash of hats and they both thought that an Easter bonnet theme to dress the windows would encourage more customers to call in. They had great fun sorting through the shelves and in the back room for eye catching millinery delights. When Madam wasn't around they would stand in front of the large costume mirror trying the hats on. Their giggling was a welcome breath of fresh air to Poppy. The story of the little gold donkey brooch and its connection to the First World War, the trenches, the huge loss of young men, cut down in their prime, had lingered. There had been much talk about the 100-year anniversary of THE GREAT WAR and for the first time in her life Poppy began to reflect upon her name and its obvious connection to *Flanders Fields*. The notion of war really bothered her, the ugliness, the devastation and all the broken pieces that were left in its wake. She recalled Ted's words, "nothing good about it."

Madam's soirees had been reduced to once a week now; the warmer weather meant less of the lonely aged needing somewhere to go. Ollie still played his heavenly harp and Cedric had become an item with his violin. Madam suggested baskets of miniature chocolate eggs on the sewing machine tables instead of the staple chocolate cakes. An old record player blasted out Bing Crosby singing *Easter Parade*, the popular song written by Irving Berlin and published in 1933. Poppy had written a little card and placed it discreetly in the window asking for vintage hats to complete their window display for Easter. The little tattered booklet called, *"The Twelve Healers,"* by Edward Bach remained untouched on the oak counter top.

A few days later Poppy arrived early one morning to be greeted by a rather large and attractive hat box waiting on the doorstep. After tidying up, sweeping the wooden floor and brewing some coffee Poppy settled down to carefully examine the contents. Amongst the layers of faded tissue paper there were a couple of very attractive hats probably from the 1950's but what really caught Poppy's eye was the attractive rubber bathing cap, covered with pink and white rubber daisy flowers with little yellow centres. There was a pink rubber chinstrap to hold it in place on the bather's head. Surprisingly the rubber bathing cap was in excellent condition and was probably quite an expensive purchase all those years ago. Poppy held it closer, shut her eyes and was taken back to another time.

Jilly was attractive. She had a mane of luscious red hair. Her skin was the colour of fine porcelain. She had a great figure, a bubbly, vivacious, popular personality, always laughing and joking and she was a swimmer. All her life she had been a water baby, her middle-class parents owned a smart restaurant in the town and a nice beach hut on the promenade at Westbrook near the Royal Sea Bathing Hospital. Jilly's grandparents had spent hours with her during the long school summer holidays at the beach hut; she had learnt to swim in the sea from an early age under grandpa's careful guidance.

When Jilly became a teenager she asked her parents if she could start swimming at the Cliftonville Lido. In the 1950's The Lido was popular, the large seawater swimming pool, with its high diving boards, was a gathering place in the summer for both the locals and the holidaymakers. Many of Jilly's friends regularly frequented the pool. The Art Deco site was also a venue for social events; an entertainment complex of cafes, concert hall, bars, bandstand and hot sea and fresh water-baths surrounded the seawater pool.

Jilly always aspired to be a competitive swimmer. She was agile and confident in the water, and she had high hopes of taking her swimming ability to greater levels. She always dreamed of swimming for the county and gaining a place on the Olympic team one day would of course be the icing on the cake. At first Jilly's parents were happy with their little girl wanting more swimming and diving lessons and entering local competitions, even paying extra for private tuition but as she became older, began to grow more mature and even more attractive, her mother clearly had other ideas.

"Upwardly mobile," was the best way to describe Jilly's mother. She was a tall, elegant lady who had worked hard in the restaurant business and her priority was that her only child should marry well. She wanted to see her in an expensive house in the best part of town, wearing designer clothes and on the arm of a successful husband. Living the life of a competitive swimmer simply didn't rate highly on her agenda. Jilly's grandpa, her best and most trusted ally, had passed away when she was 13 and there was no one in Jilly's camp to lend her moral support. Jilly's mother was difficult and dictatorial.

The Lido held bathing beauty competitions every week during the summer season. Young ladies would parade around in their swimsuits, judges would select the winners, there were prizes to be won and the local newspaper would publish their photographs. This was the place to be seen especially if you wanted to attract a man, who sometimes had honourable intentions but more often than not this was a sure way to attract trouble.

By the time Jilly was sixteen the pretty young girl was troubled. She was a sensitive soul and had always appreciated everything her parents had sacrificed and done for her. She had been sent to a good private school, her parents had paid for her swimming lessons but it had become increasing obvious that her mother was also in charge of her life. There was a price to pay. She missed her grandpa and not wanting to rock the boat she invariably wore a smile and went along with all of her mother's stupid requests because Jilly just didn't like quarrels and awkward confrontation. Sadly behind the smile however was a very tormented, restless young lady who put on a brave face and hid her troubles with good humour.

Inevitably she found herself signed up for the Lido bathing beauty contest. She was undoubtedly attractive and was a strong contender for first prize in her new elegant pink and white swimsuit. Her mother had also purchased a very expensive matching swim cap covered with pink and white daisies from a designer shop up in London. Jilly really didn't want to be there. The place, the time and the competition just didn't feel right, the whole process was ridiculous in her mind and she was extremely cross with herself for even agreeing to her mother's demands. Jilly walked onto the Lido complex with a smile on her face, her luscious red hair curled around her shoulders, the pink and white costume covering an elegant figure toned by so much swimming and her right hand carried the brand new, very expensive rubber swim cap. Her mother sat in the audience beaming.

Jilly didn't see the large plastic beach ball that young Joey had thrown up onto the poolside because in her mind she was angry and elsewhere. She tripped and fell hitting her head very hard and badly injuring her back as she struck the side of the concrete pool. She wasn't party to all the commotion that followed as it took her several days to regain consciousness. After a few days in Margate General Hospital she was transferred to The Royal Sea Bathing Hospital, the hospital's orthopaedic expertise and the skills of the medical staff eventually nursed her back to health again but Jilly's days as a competitive swimmer were over.

Eventually, to please her parents, Jilly married a successful businessman and the couple became well known in the town for their grand parties. She had a family of her own but in her quiet moments she always reflected on what could have been, the dreams that were never fulfilled and the true happiness that she never quite realized as she lived out someone else's dream. She took to drinking more than her fair share of gin and tonics and fine wines just to keep a smile and good humour on her face but deep down she felt tormented and angry. Occasionally she would pull the rubber bathing cap out and cry. She had never been able to pass it on. It was a timely reminder of a lovely young girl who never got her own wish and followed her own path. As Jilly grew much older she lost her good looks and the excess alcohol and high living led to a number of debilitating health problems. Eventually, several years after Jilly's death, her own daughter bundled the swimming cap up into a hat box along with some other items and left it on Madam's doorstep after she had seen Poppy's discreet note in the shop window.

Poppy opened her eyes and looked down at the chic pink and white bathing cap. It didn't quite hold the same allure that she had felt when it had first been pulled out of the hat box. The story struck a chord in Poppy's heart, she could feel Jilly's pain and the anguish that she had felt because her dreams had never reached realization. Jilly had lived someone else's dream and in doing so had evaded true happiness. Poppy sighed, she knew many people whose stories matched Jilly's. Poppy pondered on all the things that had happened since she had become gainfully employed at the Madam Popoff Vintage Emporium. She had become privy to so many peoples stories, some good, some tragic and some particularly unsettling. Poppy had honed her fingering skills; she could feel energy, comprehend ownership and sense stories. She had learnt a lot about herself and then there were the goings on in the back room, this was something else that needed further investigation.

The back room, like Aunt Flora's Lookout Retreat, was a cavernous place. Ollie's heavenly harp took up much of the space in one of the corners. Madam told him it was far too big and cumbersome to take back and forth every time there was a soiree so he was allowed to leave it in the back room. Ollie had a number of harps at his home. Fellow musicians had "fallen off the perch," as Uncle Bertie liked to say, and their harp was usually bequeathed to Ollie. There were large numbers of boxes and several costume rails filled with clothes waiting to be sorted and priced before graduating to the shop floor. In another corner stood a kitchen sink, worktop, an old electric stove and there was shelving above stacked with oddly matched porcelain cups, saucers and plates waiting to grace the sewing machine tables at the soirees. There were a number of old biscuit tins waiting for the chocolate cake and other shelves and cupboards were filled with gift boxes, wrapping paper, coloured ribbon and all sorts of odds and ends. In another corner a number of chairs were stacked waiting for the next soiree along with the sewing machine tables rescued from Scott's Emporium. In the centre of it all were two comfortable armchairs, very old and worn but covered with bright blue chintz covers and adorned with plump red cushions. A little coffee table stood nearby. When Madam Popoff made an appearance she often spent a lot of time in one of the armchairs.

Looking back, over the many months that Poppy had worked at the shop, she had come to realize that a large number of customers and browsers had actually been invited into the back room. Madam would take their hand as she talked to them on the shop floor and would gently say, "Come." There was a lot more going on in the shop than Poppy had originally thought. People seemed to spend hours talking to Madam. She kept a box of tissues on the coffee table and occasionally Poppy would hear the whistle of the kettle as Madam made a cup of tea and offered chocolate cake. Madam had remarked once that chocolate helped mend broken hearts and many times she would say to Poppy, "To dress and mend the broken pieces, that's what we do here, Poppy."

"To mend the broken pieces," Poppy muttered to Jack the Lad as she cycled on the promenade from Cliftonville past the derelict Lido complex towards Margate harbour. This was yet another one of Aunt Flora's blot on the landscape sites. In present times there were a lot of broken pieces to be seen. Sadly, the once thriving, popular Lido bathing complex, was mostly abandoned and neglected. It was clearly unloved and a shameful mess. The main pool, now filled with sand and concrete, was windswept by sand, the occasional clump of grass had taken root and rubbish had accumulated. As Poppy looked around the pitiful site she felt total despair. The lovely Lido buildings at the pool level were currently falling apart and plastered over with offensive graffiti. This once very pleasant and attractive facility had taken on a distinctively, "seedy aura." Poppy didn't want to linger here, the nostalgia of the good times in the past had left, and it was all so ugly. Time had moved on and now Poppy only saw a wasted landscape of desolation, darkness and death. The Lido's fortunes on the pool level had changed; now it was a place where drunks, druggies and others, "up to no good" often gathered.

"Back in 2008 The Lido was granted a preservation order giving it a Grade 2 listing so it had been given a level of protection as a site of historical significance and could not be built upon by one of those opportunistic housing developers," remarked Aunt Flora as she sat with Poppy at the dining table that evening.

"I remember it all so well; originally it was known as The Clifton Baths Estate. It was at the Lido where I first met Uncle Bertie. We were young and so in love, I was a good swimmer in those days and I used to enter the lovely legs competitions. I won a few times, I recall the judges giving me boxes of chocolates and a vanity bag. I do hope that one day the right person will come along, purchase the Lido and restore it to its former glory. It deserves to be loved again, its present fate is so unfair." Poppy sighed as she reflected upon the circle of life, and the recognition that fortunes follow both people and places. Living is so full of ups and downs, the good times, the bad times and the ugly times are all part of the rich tapestry of human existence.

Chapter 18

"One of the prettiest theatres we have ever seen."
Keble's Margate and Ramsgate Gazette

May had arrived and Margate was becoming busier, the warm weather and bright blue skies brought crowds of day trippers down from London and coach loads of pensioners arrived on early season bargain breaks. Madam decided to stop the soirées, the shop had become much busier with the influx of visitors and it was agreed that they would resume again in late October when the weather closed in.

A large antique wooden steamer trunk had arrived a few days ago. Two young lads carried it down into the Old Town from Addington Street and Margate's Theatre Royal. The theatre had originally opened in 1787 and was notoriously known to be one of Southern England's most haunted theatres.

"All kinds of things supposedly go on there, flashing lights, footsteps, thuds on the floor, a stage curtain that moves on its own and even a clock with hands that go backwards in time!" Exclaimed Isadora when the two young lads announced where they had come from.

Apparently The Theatre Royal was having a wash and brush up before the season got too busy. Workmen had been brought in to do some electrical repairs up in the attic and Alan and his lads had found the old trunk wedged up in the rafters and resting on some old wiring. The theatre's management decided that it was simply packed with old costumes with nothing of much value and had asked Alan to dispose of it. He had mentioned it to his wife whose elderly father happened to be a regular attendee at Madam's soirées so it was decided that Madam would inherit the trunk. At least it spared Alan a trip to the Margate Tip.

The old wooden trunk housed an interesting mix of clothes, wigs and theatrical props but most of them were very old and musty and of little appeal. Poppy volunteered to carefully sift through the contents and determine what could be salvaged. There were a couple of late Victorian dresses in need of repair work, a few pairs of gloves and a hat, all in good enough condition to earn a place on the shop floor but sadly the rest of the contents weren't suitable for sale, damp, mould and moths had got to them.

Poppy went into the back room and brought out a black dustbin liner, she began to put the mouldy items into the bag but when she came to a very big, old battered ladies black leather bag she opened it to ensure nothing was hidden inside. To her surprise out fell a beautiful theatre mask the sort you see for sale in the shops around Venice. The large thick leather bag had protected it and it was truly beautiful. "Oh my," gasped Poppy as she fingered the Venetian white and gold papier-mâché mask with a jester's headpiece crafted from thick, stiff ribbons in various shades of purple and decorated with little silver bells. As Poppy muttered to herself, "This must surely have a story to tell," she looked at the old wall clock just above Madam's large costume mirror and could have sworn that the hands were actually turning backwards.

With one eye on the tea kettle and the other on her own watch so she could compare the time with the old clock above the costume mirror Poppy was all a fluster and eager to sit down with her cuppa and examine the mask. It was near closing time and Poppy had decided to flip the sign in the door window and settle down to investigate further. As her fingers moved gently over the beautifully crafted mask she was transported back to another time.

It was the summer of 1885 and Albert was extremely lucky; his wealthy family packed him off to Margate and the first established drama school in the country. Sarah Thorne, a well-known actress and manager of the Theatre Royal, had opened the School of Acting a few years back. Sarah came from a theatrical family. Her father; reputedly an effeminate man with a passion for gambling, had become the theatre manager in 1855 and at the age of 18 young Sarah had made her acting debut as *Pauline* in Lord Lytton's verse drama. Sarah took over as manager in 1861.

The Theatre Royal, sited at the northeast corner of Hawley Square, and acknowledged as one of the oldest theatres in the United Kingdom had undergone a significant conversion in 1874 and had evolved from a Georgian Boxed Playhouse into a Victorian Theatre. It welcomed some of the greatest stars of the Victorian era. Margate's proud heritage of being one of the first seaside resorts, founded on the craze for sea bathing, was a popular place and often frequented by well to do people who enjoyed the theatre and could well afford to purchase a seat.

Albert, a gregarious, clever and ambitious young man, had one mission in life. He had always wanted to act and he knew full well that he had the gift, he had been the star performer in many school plays and he had regularly entertained his wealthy family at their large mansion and vast country estate when he returned home from his elite public school for the holidays. His headmaster wasn't too pleased when young Albert declared, near the end of term, that he wouldn't be going up to Oxford or Cambridge because he was off to Margate and the newly established acting school. Several gasps of horror had echoed around the staff common room.

Albert was definitely a fortunate young man because his loving parents agreed to humour their only son and his acting ambitions. "It's a passing whim," grunted his father, "he'll soon get fed up with Margate and theatre people and he'll go up to university a year later, I'm sure."

Albert arrived in Margate and took a couple of rooms in a large Georgian boarding house on nearby Victoria Road. Sarah Thorne was quite a taskmaster but he settled comfortably into theatre life. Albert honed his skills and his enthusiasm for drama was infectious. He was very popular with peer group and public alike; these were happy, productive days. Albert enjoyed all that Margate had to offer particularly the seaside, clean, fresh air and the bathing machines provided by Mr Edward Perkins on Margate sands. Of course, best of all, was the theatre lifestyle. Sarah called her little troupe her *pupes* and Albert was her most flamboyant, fun loving, and talented young student, although almost too enthusiastic.

Time passed quickly, Albert began to earn his own money and became less financially reliant upon his father's support. It became increasingly clear through his enthusiastic letters home that he loved Margate and wasn't showing any remorse at all for choosing acting school above Oxford or Cambridge. "Give him more time," urged his mother in her attempts to calm her anxious husband, "he'll come round and go in a year or two."

There was only one thing that gnawed away at Albert's happiness, his growing realization that he had homosexual leanings. Being in the company of theatre people together with some past experiences from his days as a public schoolboy had brought all this to the surface and now he didn't really know what to do. He was thankful that he wasn't anywhere near his loving family who would never have condoned such a lifestyle. His family would have been horrified if they discovered the truth, such tendencies would bring shame and embarrassment to the family name. In Margate Albert was anonymous and within the closeted theatrical community there were many other young men hiding illicit liaisons.

Margate was a place of secrets; Albert knew full well the stiff penalties that could be enforced if his sexual exploits were ever discovered. He could be tried as a criminal and it wasn't unusual to be sent to prison for a few years. It had only been back in 1861 that the death sentence for such behaviour was repealed. So when Sarah Thorne announced that she would be taking her theatre troupe on tour to Italy for several months in the early part of 1887 Albert breathed a sigh of relief. He would be out of England during the coldest months of the year, even further away from people who knew him and this was a marvellous opportunity to travel and take in the sights and sounds of exotic places, destinations he had only visited in his dreams.

Masquerade masks, associated with Venice Carnival, had been a popular form of disguise for a long time both in England and Europe. They had many uses including hiding ones identity, expressing one's freedom of speech and voicing one's emotions and opinions without judgment. Albert decided that when he was in Italy he would try to seek out and purchase his own lovely mask and he looked forward to his trip abroad with relish.

The Festival of Venice Carnival, a centuries old tradition, originally began on December 26th and ended with *Mardi Gras.* Supposedly it all started in 1162 when Venice celebrated its victory over the Patriarch of Aquileia. It was a time when the rigid social hierarchy of the Venetian Republic let down its hair and relieved pent up tension; people could have fun, peasants and aristocrats mixed as their true social class identity was hidden under a mask. The town filled with entertainers, there was music, dancing, and plays. Heavy drinking and inevitably debauchery and promiscuous activity followed. During the Carnival time people could be free. Sadly, it was also a time when a masquerader could take the opportunity to commit criminal offences such as murder, robbery and indecent acts. Masks conferred anonymity and anyone could be who they wanted to be, they could gamble, indulge in illicit and clandestine affairs and pursue their own fancies. A close relationship between the theatre and the carnival soon developed and all kinds of theatrical activities were organized in both private and public places during carnival time. However, this all came to an end when Napoleon Bonaparte sent Austrian invaders and the Venetian Republic fell. It was no longer independent and the Carnival was banned. The last Carnival reportedly happened in 1797.

Albert knew that the Carnival no longer took place in Venice but there had been many whispers of masked parties and balls still happening in private Venetian homes and palaces. He hoped that during some of their time in Italy he would have an opportunity to experience this flamboyant, exotic lifestyle and to acquire his own mask. Sarah Thorne's theatrical troupe had a number of engagements booked as their planned train journey made its way across Europe to Venice. After taking the steamship from Dover to Calais where they stayed for a week performing, they continued by train and stopped for varying amounts of time in Paris, Lausanne and Milan before reaching their final destination. Albert kept a journal of all their exploits, the sights, sounds and smells of all the towns and cities that they visited and the varying successes of their theatrical performances.

Albert, as always, captivated his audiences with his natural talent and his flamboyant flair. The dashing young man caught the eye of all the ladies who loved him but it was the young men who came to watch that caught Albert's eye and his desire.

The troupe had been travelling for two months before they finally reached Venice. The beautiful city smelled bad, a rank odour permeated the narrow streets and waterways. They were all disappointed. Sarah organized a few performances at Venetian theatres and they had been invited to entertain at some private parties. It was the parties that Albert most looked forward to. They had plenty of spare time to explore the narrow streets and take some gondola rides. It was in a well-hidden, narrow side street in the bowels of the city that Albert found a small artisan workshop with a shop counter. He ventured inside and a sea of colourful masks greeted him, some black and others white, all of them exotic and beautifully crafted out of porcelain, leather or papier-mâché. The alluring masks beckoned to Albert; the ancient workshop had survived the banning of the Venice Carnival nearly a hundred years ago and currently catered exclusively to the aristocracy and their private masquerade parties.

One particular mask called to Albert, it was white and gold with beautiful stiffened purple ribbons and little silver bells. He knew this was his mask. He breathed a sigh of relief when he saw the price, he had enough money in his pocket .The mask was carefully wrapped in brown paper and tied with string and Albert carried it carefully back to their boarding house. The mask and Albert became inseparable. It became his faithful party companion both in Italy and when he eventually returned to Margate. Albert attended a lot of parties; he was popular and highly promiscuous. The mask helped to hide his deep secrets and his true identity. He had many lovers and it was only in the safety of the bedroom that he took the mask off.

Albert and his beautiful Venetian mask had been back in Margate for a year; Sarah Thorne had begun to privately worry about her bright young student who had arrived in Margate with so much promise. His partying had become excessive. He was bringing some undesirable characters into her beloved theatre and he had begun to lose both his acting edge and his youthful energy. Albert was often tired and irritable. Fellow actors began to complain, he just wasn't fun to be around any longer. He would often complain about headaches, muscle aches, sore throats and flu-like symptoms.

Sarah actually felt relieved when a letter from his mother arrived one day requesting Albert's urgent return home. His father had suffered a heart attack and a stroke and wasn't expected to live more than a week or two. Albert was needed at home and it was anticipated that he would inherit the family's vast country estate and everyone expected him to fill his father's shoes. The estate employed many servants and farm workers who all depended upon being gainfully employed, Albert would have considerable responsibility sitting on his youthful shoulders. His theatre days were over.

Of course Albert was reluctant to leave Margate and his libertine lifestyle. He had really loved acting and all that the Theatre Royal had offered him but he had loved his Venetian mask more and in some ways it had become his downfall. As he bade his goodbyes he asked Sarah to take care of his beautiful white and gold mask with its purple ribbons and silver bells. He knew he couldn't take such a thing home. Sarah didn't like its energy but neither did she have the heart to throw it away. She stuffed it in an old leather bag and hid it away in a large trunk in the theatre's attic where it lay quite forgotten.

Albert, being the only son and heir, was welcomed home with open arms. His father passed over peacefully a few days after his homecoming. His mother breathed a sigh of relief; her beloved son was now home and would continue to manage their large estate. There were many expectations to fulfil, the most prominent being marriage and producing an heir. Albert had become an expert at hiding his deep dark secret;

Margate and his mask had given him the anonymity that had enabled him to live a decadent life of excess and sexual pleasure. Times had changed now and he was expected to be a pillar of respectability. If anyone discovered the secrets of his wayward past there would be quite a scandal so Albert never did confess to his bride to be. He kept his past hidden away in the recesses of his own mind just as his Venetian mask was kept locked away in an old steamer trunk up in the rafters of the Theatre Royal.

A few years later Albert reluctantly married Fleur; she was beautiful, young and innocent. Fleur came from a prominent county family and fitted everyone's expectations of a suitable wife for Albert and the prospective mother of his children. They had a son and then Albert seemed to lose interest, he told her that he needed to sleep in his own bedroom, he made excuses but the real reason was his failing health.

Albert had thought nothing of the nagging sore throats, muscle aches and flu-like symptoms but now he was concerned about his failing mental health and he had finally decided to consult with a prominent medical doctor up in London. Of course the diagnosis of Syphilis was devastating, but confirmed Albert's own suspicion. The doctor's careful questioning about Albert's wayward past confirmed the worst. His own young son was a sickly child, he had deformed teeth, bone problems and he failed to thrive. "Congenital Syphilis occurs when a foetus is infected in the womb," announced the doctor, "sins of the fathers," he muttered glaring up at Albert. Albert's prognosis was grim as the disease was now so advanced.

Albert carried on for a couple of years, doing his best to oversee his vast country estate, he was careful to put his affairs in order. He knew that a mental asylum lay at the end of the road and he knew that when the time came and he still had his wits about him that he would kill himself. Albert never found the courage to tell his family about his past transgressions, and Syphilis remained his secret. There were to be no confessions or apologies. Eventually, just before his death he wrote to Sarah Thorne, thanking her for the time that he had spent in Margate, as they were some of the happiest days of his life. He finally admitted to Sarah that he should have made better choices when it came to finding love, he finally acknowledged that his excesses and selfish ways had brought nothing but trouble to himself and to a wider circle of people in his life, some of them being innocent bystanders who were simply in the wrong place at the wrong time.

Of course his mother and Fleur knew deep down in their hearts that Albert was very sick. A kind friend had taken Fleur aside and urged her to take their son to a homeopathic doctor in London and have him treat them both. Fleur was a deeply religious woman; she had a lovely shrine erected to The Virgin Mary. It gracefully rested in the hollowed out trunk of an oak tree high up on the hill in woods behind the great house. She would go there and pray every day for her family, particularly for their young innocent son. With the homeopath's help and Fleur's prayers the two grew strong and Fleur eventually found true love much later in life and she remarried. Albert was buried up in the woods behind the great house under the oak tree where the shrine had been erected. His elderly mother would often go there and weep.

Sarah had continued to guide the fortunes of the Theatre Royal until 1894 and then it began to decline. The Sarah Thorne Theatre Company had secured a seven-year lease on the Opera House in Chatham as well as a second home in that town for Sarah. She passed away there aged 62 on 27th February 1899, having contracted influenza and never recovered. As for Albert's Venetian mask, it remained hidden in the old leather handbag; it was stuffed away in the steamer trunk at The Theatre Royal.

Poppy opened her eyes and looked down at the beautiful Venetian mask with stiffened purple ribbons and little silver bells she was crying. It was such a sad story but somehow the captivating mask had drawn her in and she felt that she couldn't pass it onto Madam and her allotment bonfire it was just too lovely to burn. She placed it on the shelf next to the little gold donkey brooch with the seed pearl eye; the same shelf where once the exquisite beaded clutch bag with irises blowing in the wind had waited patiently for the Parker girl. It was late and she locked up.

The next day when Madam made an appearance and she looked up at the mask, her wizened face said it all. She was disappointed in Poppy but Madam knew that she had come to the shop to learn lessons so the mask must stay awhile. Madam glided by and went into the back room to brew some tea.

It only took a couple of weeks for Poppy to realize that all was not well in the shop. A number of very grumpy customers complained about various things this had never happened before. One lady tripped over the threshold and badly cut her knee, another lady fell down the single stair by the door, and a few costume jewellery items had been pilfered. Poppy's throat was sore, she felt that she might be going down with a summer cold and Isadora had developed a bad cough. The doctor told her to stay in bed for a few days. Even Jack the Lad was unhappy, for the first time ever he and Winston exchanged some irritable growls and Winston was off his sausages. Mary said he had a bad tummy. Poppy looked up at the mask, the face seemed to be watching all the comings and goings in the shop and for the first time she noticed that the little gold donkey brooch with the seed pearl eye had moved away and was cowering in the far corner of the shelf.

Poppy had a restless night and decided that she really must hand the mask over to Madam; she finally admitted to herself that it couldn't be sold and be passed onto someone else to cause trouble. Poppy rose early and decided to forgo her usual cycle ride to Ramsgate and Ship Shape Café for breakfast. She planned to arrive early and sort things out in the shop and wait for Madam. To her surprise the shop door was open and careful examination indicated that the lock had been picked. Poppy rushed in and anxiously checked the till and looked around to see what was missing. After several hours of searching she came to the conclusion that everything was in tact except for the Venetian mask, the old steamer trunk, stored in the back room, the two Victorian dresses, gloves and hat, in fact all the things that Poppy had salvaged when Alan's lads dropped the trunk off at Madam's shop a few weeks ago.

93

When she finally sat down with a cup of coffee and began to take stock of the whole situation she looked up and noticed that the little gold donkey brooch with the seed pearl eye was sitting in the middle of the shelf and glowing brightly. Poppy looked around. She could feel the change. Everything in the shop seemed to glow. There was an aura of peace and happiness, almost as if a big dark cloud had lifted and drifted off and out through the door.

Madam eventually made an appearance, she seemed happier and gave Poppy a gentle hug. She didn't say much simply, "I'll call Ollie and Cedric and ask if they'll bring their toolkit to fix that lock on the front door." Nothing else was said, Poppy knew she had made a mistake, she had let the mask draw her in and it had caused nothing but trouble. She resolved that she would make wiser decisions in the future. "All that glitters is not always gold, I've been such a fool," Poppy confided to Jack the Lad as later that day they went for a bike ride along the prom. Poppy never really questioned the break-in. She had recalled the time on Christmas Eve when she had stopped outside the forever Christmas house and Madam had appeared. Poppy had learnt that sometimes it wasn't for us to ask questions and sometimes it wasn't for us to know the answers.

That evening, back at Lookout Retreat, over dinner, Aunt Flora was in her element, she had always loved the theatre and enjoyed filling Poppy in with the history of Margate's Theatre Royal, the ebb and flow of its fortunes and all about the ghost of Sarah Thorne. "The theatre has had so many mixed fortunes over the years, of course I'm more familiar with its history in the 20th century. I do know that it was closed during the First World War. Actually, it was purchased in 1915 by the famous Margate department store Bobby and Co. and it was used as a warehouse until the 1920's when it was eventually closed. It opened up again as a theatre in 1930 and then closed again during the Second World War. Since then it has had a lot of ups and downs. Eventually it was fully closed in 1965 but was saved from demolition by becoming a bingo hall and by being granted listed building status. Currently it is a Grade 2 listed building. *The Theatre Royal Trust* took over full ownership in 2002 and as you know Poppy, it hosts plenty of theatrical happenings. Uncle Bertie and I were always keen supporters."

Poppy looked up from eating her dessert and asked, "What about all the hauntings that people speak about?" Aunt Flora sighed, "Yes, they do say that much of that sort of thing began in 1918. The restless ghost of Sarah Thorne was first seen, apparently to protest at the modern use of her beloved theatre firstly as a furniture store then as a bingo and gambling hall. Certainly, a lot of strange happenings have been documented, an orange ball of light, screams, heavy footsteps, a clock whose hands move backwards. In more recent times an electrician swears that Sarah glided down the stairs past him one day and disappeared, at first he thought that it was one of the performers in Victorian costume but then he realized that the theatre had been locked up and only he and a colleague were on the site."

As she lay in bed that night Poppy pondered over many things. She thought about Sarah, her beloved theatre and her restless spirit. She thought about Albert and how his irresponsible ways had brought nothing but trouble and heartbreak. She recalled that it was during the Margate Gay Parade that she had first found her way into Madam's shop. She thought about the passage of time and what the rainbow flag stood for. She was happy that society was generally much more tolerant and accepting and that such relationships could now be openly displayed but she couldn't condone Albert's promiscuity this had brought nothing but tragedy. Poppy was beginning to fully understand the relationship between people and places, the things that they owned, their hopes and dreams, the mistakes that we all make and how our actions can have devastating repercussions for generations to come. Reflecting back on some of the things that she had grown to truly love in the shop, particularly the iris bag and the little donkey brooch, she thought about the much finer qualities of selfless love and courage. As she drifted off to sleep her mind turned to Ted Parker and the crew of *The Lord Southborough,* noble men who risked their own lives for those of strangers.

Chapter 19

When Poppy arrived to open up the shop the next day she was at long last drawn to the tattered booklet by Edward Bach, *"The Twelve Healers,"* it had sat upon the oak countertop gathering dust for quite sometime. Poppy made herself a cup of coffee and in the quietness of the early morning she knew that the time had come to give this her full attention. The student was ready. She began to read. The opening lines were so intriguing:

"This system of treatment is the most perfect which has been given to mankind within living memory. It has the power to cure disease, and, in its simplicity, it may be used in the household."

As Poppy continued to read she learnt that the system of healing set out in the little booklet had been Divinely revealed, a Gift from God, and showed that our fears, our cares, our anxieties, likes and dislikes, greed, indecision and such like are the things that open the path to the invasion of illness. Poppy learnt that the Herbs given to us by the Grace of the Creator could take away the fears and worries and would leave us happier and better in ourselves and in doing so the disease, no matter what it is, would leave.

"The remedies of Nature given in this book have proved that that they are blest above others in their work of mercy; and that they have been given the power to heal all types of illness and suffering."

As Poppy continued to read she became more and more interested. She knew so many sick people up in London and even more now that she had come to Margate. Many customers who crossed the threshold of the Madam Popoff Vintage Emporium had some sort of ailment. However, over the past year Poppy noticed that those who spent time in the back room with Madam seemed to do a lot better. In fact so many returned just to thank Madam that Poppy began to wonder if Madam knew all about this system of healing introduced by Edward Bach.

"Take no notice of the disease, think only of the outlook on life of the one in distress."

Poppy began to understand that it was important to treat the personality and not the disease. Treat the state of mind or the moods and with the return to normal, the disease, whatever it might be, would go away too. Poppy found this all to be extremely fascinating. She had become privy to so many life stories during her sojourn at the Madam Popoff Vintage Emporium and now she was learning how people could be helped in their sufferings. She knew so many people who had undergone counselling over the years, including herself, but still remained stuck in their own traumas, dramas and sickness. Poppy smiled to herself. Edward Bach had arrived to open a new door in her life and Poppy was about to embark upon a whole new adventure!

The little booklet continued to describe *"The Twelve Healers"* and recommended the following herbs:

* ***Agrimony*** for cheerful people who like to joke and laugh and cannot cope with arguments or quarrels, these are carefully avoided, they worry and can feel restless and tormented by their troubles but these are always carefully hidden behind good humour. They tend to use alcohol and drugs to help them keep up the façade of cheerfulness.

Jilly and the pretty bathing cap with the pink and white daisies with the yellow centres immediately came to mind. Jilly had been a people pleaser. She didn't like confrontation and quarrels and went along with her mother's demands, keeping a smile and good humour on her face. Poppy reflected upon the bathing beauty contest at the Lido and how Jilly had tripped and taken a very bad fall, sadly her future as a competitive swimmer was over in an instant. Poppy recalled how Jilly liked to party later in life. She had drowned her sorrows in plenty of alcohol and eventually passed away from lots of health problems attributed to a less than healthy lifestyle. Poppy wondered if *Agrimony* would have been a good remedy for Jilly.

* *Centaury* would apparently be beneficial for quiet, gentle people who are over anxious to help and serve other people and whose good nature often results in them doing much more than their fair share of the work, so much so that they may neglect their own mission in life.

Poppy saw many aspects of this remedy in her own life story. She had always wanted to help others. She knew it was important to be kind and helpful, after all they were such noble traits. She had always been taught this growing up, but she did realize that other people had perceived her weakness and her inability to set healthy boundaries. Consequently many had taken advantage. Poppy knew that she found it very difficult to say, "NO" and realized that her own weakness had set herself up for situations that caused her grief, anger and festering resentment.

Poppy also remembered the beautiful Valentine's ball gown, Edna and Bill's story. She recalled how Edna was so sweet and nice and did a lot to please her mother to her own disadvantage.

* *Cerato* for those who don't have sufficient confidence in themselves to make their own decisions, constantly ask advice from others and are often misguided.

Poppy could see aspects of this remedy matched her own personality and also that of Edna. When Bill had asked for Edna's hand in marriage at the Dreamland dance, she hadn't been able to answer him. She needed time to think and decide, and had worried about leaving her mother until it was all too late and Bill had died in Korea.

* *Chicory* for those who are over mindful of the needs of others and tend to be over full of care for children, relatives and friends. They are always trying to find something to put right. They are possessive people, they want their loved ones near and enjoy correcting things they consider wrong. They are apt to become fussy and agitated in their care for others.

Poppy immediately thought about Edna's mother who had seemed very possessive and didn't like the fact that Edna had a boyfriend and definitely not a Yank; her big fear was that she might be whisked far away to America! Edna's story was so sad; she had spent the rest of her life looking after her mother, tied to her apron strings.

* ***Clematis*** could be recommended for those who are dreamy, drowsy, and not fully awake and who have no great interest in life. Quiet people, who are not really happy in their present circumstances, live more in the future than in the present. In illness some make little effort to get well, and in certain cases may even look forward to death because they might meet again some loved one whom they have lost.

Poppy smiled and immediately thought about Ted and all the time that he had spent up at the donkey stables avoiding his father and the chaos at home. Ted would dream of far off places and adventures. He always seemed to be somewhere else. He had found it difficult to pay attention at school because of his daydreaming and when he came home his mother would tell him to get his feet on the ground and help out. Maybe he had needed some *Clematis.*

* ***Gentian*** for those who are easily discouraged. They may be progressing well in illness or in the affairs of their daily life but don't do well if there is a small delay or hindrance to progress, as they soon become doubtful and disheartened.

Poppy's thoughts turned to The Royal Sea Bathing Hospital and Johnny's story; he was so despondent when Alf had first visited, she smiled and pictured the jaunty little Superman doll, it was the doll and Alf's love and dedication that turned him around but maybe *Gentian* would have helped too. Then there had been little Angus who arrived in the shop on Christmas Eve. Angus had been so despondent. Poppy shed a tear when she saw the little boy in her mind. He had turned his head away when she had asked about Father Christmas. He had bit his lip and tried hard not to cry. Surely he would have benefited from this remedy.

* *Impatiens* for those who are quick in thought and action and who wish all things to be done without hesitation or delay. When they are ill they are anxious for a hasty recovery. They don't like slow people and they often prefer to work alone so that they can get everything done at their own speed.

Well, Poppy knew many people who probably needed this particular remedy! She reflected upon some of her colleagues up in London. She thought about some of the customers who had crossed the threshold of the Madam Popoff Vintage Emporium. Eventually her mind turned to Jack the Lad. He was always so impatient, always urging her onto Ramsgate, Ship Shape Café, Winston and the sausages. Poppy wondered if these remedies would be good for animals too.

* *Mimulus* for those who are fearful. It is for the fear of everyday life, of worldly things such as illness, pain, accidents, poverty, of the dark, of being alone, and of misfortune. These people quietly keep these things to themselves and don't speak about their fears to others.

Poppy knew this would also be a good remedy for herself, so many of her friends told her that she needed more courage especially in the love department! Poppy suddenly recalled that she had heard this name before; of course Madam had pointed out the little yellow flowers on Edna's ball gown and commented that they were called *Mimulus*. Edna needed courage too, she had been a fearful lady, fearful of leaving home, fearful of leaving her mother and fearful about following Bill to America. Poppy felt that Edna might have benefited from this remedy.

* *Rock Rose* the remedy for emergency, where there appears to be no hope. In accident or sudden illness, or when the patient is very frightened or terrified.

Poppy immediately thought about Ted out there in no man's land with the other lads. They had been lost and knew that if they didn't make it back by first light they would all be done for. Surely they would have all needed *Rock Rose?* Ted didn't have Bach remedies at that time but he did have his own special angel, his little gold donkey brooch with its seed pearl eye, which kept him calm and told him to look to the stars for help.

* ***Scleranthus*** for those who suffer much from being unable to decide between two things, first one seeming right then the other. They are usually quiet people, and bear their difficulty alone, as they are not inclined to discuss it with others.

Poppy's thoughts once again turned to her own situation, for it had taken her a very long time to eventually make up her mind and decide to come to Margate. She had toyed with the idea for a long time and just wished that she had done it years ago!

* ***Vervain*** for those with fixed principles and ideas, which they are confident are right, and which they rarely change. They have a great wish to convert all those around to their own views of life. They have a strong will and like to teach. This is a remedy for over enthusiasm and a strained state of mind.

Poppy immediately thought about Albert and his acting career, he had a very strong will, he was extremely enthusiastic and maybe too much so for his own good. His passionate lifestyle had in the end become his downfall and precipitated an untimely death. She wondered if this remedy might have brought a sense of calm and balance to his life, a realization that all the numerous affairs might not be the best path to follow.

* ***Water Violet*** for those who in health and illness like to be alone. Very quiet people who move about without noise, speak little and then gently. They are very independent, capable and self-reliant and almost free of the opinions of others. They are aloof, leave people alone and go their own way. Water Violet types are often clever and talented. Their peace and calmness is a blessing to those around them.

Poppy sighed; she could see so many of her friends, the customers at the Madam Popoff Vintage Emporium, people from her past, herself included in these remedy pictures. Then there were so many of the people whose lives had come to her through the things that she had handled in the shop, at one time or another they too may have benefited from one or more of these *"Twelve Healers."*

She put the little tattered book back on the oak counter top and knew that she needed to learn more about Dr. Bach and his remedies. Poppy wondered if she had found her most important treasure.

Chapter 20

Dancing was on her mind when Poppy opened up the shop one bright Monday in early June. Aunt Flora had invited her to a tea dance at The Winter Gardens up on Fort Crescent on Sunday afternoon. Poppy wasn't much of a dancer but she loved to talk with Flora's friends, all elegant ladies and elderly gentlemen with silver hair who loved to dress up, socialize and dance. They always had such fascinating stories to tell. An ancient suitcase, plastered with bright luggage labels from a bygone era, had been left by the front door with a post it note instructing Madam Popoff to use what she could and to kindly throw the rest away. Poppy went about her usual duties sweeping the floor, tidying up, washing the cups in the back room and getting ready for a busy day. The town was filling with tourists now and business had picked up.

Poppy eventually settled down with a cup of coffee. It was still early and no customers had stepped across the threshold yet so she decided to investigate and open up the suitcase. A few old clothes spilled out, they smelled musty and didn't hold much appeal, "Someone has been up in their attic spring-cleaning," sighed Poppy. However, as she dug deeper she discovered a few pairs of old but really pretty dancing shoes probably dating from the 1930-1940's and she knew that Madam would be interested in these. As she dug deeper what really captivated her attention was a beautiful heart shaped wooden box wrapped in layers of faded, yellowing tissue paper. It looked as if it was made of cherry or some other close grained wood and inlaid with mother of pearl. Two tiny glass swans sat on top and when she carefully opened the lid she could see that it was a musical jewellery box. Poppy fiddled with the key at the back and much to her surprise a tune began to play. She recognized Tchaikovsky's *Swan Lake*. Poppy smiled, gently held the box and whilst she listened to the music and the box lay close to her heart she drifted off to another time.

Bunty was a pretty young thing only 17 years old but already with a couple of competitive dancing awards under her belt. She was very good at ballroom and when she had stayed with relatives up in London for a few months during the spring of 1914 a wealthy aunt paid for her to take ballet lessons. "Fidgety feet," called her doting father as she swanned out of the front door. Bunty never seemed to be still for very long, she was always in a hurry, busy and impatient much of the time. Tonight she was running late for the end of summer competition at The Winter Gardens Ballroom. She had been held up at The Hotel Metropole, a large hotel standing at the landward end of the Margate Jetty. It was popular with the visitors who arrived by steamship. Bunty had recently taken a job as a housekeeper but because she was a bright, well-educated girl she often helped out at the reception desk. Monty, her dancing partner, would be cross that she was so late. They made a lovely couple, completely dedicated to each other and to their dancing. They dreamed of owning a ballroom dancing school one day in the future. Dancing was becoming more and more popular especially in holiday resorts like Margate and they both had keen business minds. It was early days yet but they both predicted that dancing and a school would be their future. They were bright young stars with a sparkly future ahead of them.

That evening, once they were both out on the dance floor, they excelled. Bunty and Monty moved through the Waltz and the newly introduced Fox Trot, all the way from America, with the precision and accuracy of a Swiss watch. The judges couldn't find fault with their naturally youthful talent, they were two young people in perfect harmony. As first prize winners that evening Bunty was presented with a beautiful heart shaped box crafted from cherry and inlaid with mother of pearl. The mother of pearl was in the shape of a pond and two tiny glass swans sat on top. As she carefully opened the lid she realized that it was a musical box and when she turned the key clockwork swans circled the pond to the sweet notes of *Swan Lake*. "My what a treasure!" Exclaimed Bunty. Monty received an equally lovely matching oblong box crafted from the same wood, the mother of pearl, inlaid in the lid, cast the single image of a swan. "Oh," he gasped and as he opened it he could see it was a special case holding a fountain pen.

This dancing competition was to be the last time that the couple competed together. The future was uncertain; war had recently broken out in Europe and many of the Margate lads talked about joining up. Monty worked for Mr Edward Perkins and his Bathing Machine and Furniture Removal Company down on Margate's Marine Sands. Monty had a gift for figures and kept Mr Perkins accounting books in perfect order. He was very friendly with many of the donkey boys who also worked down on the sands. In the past they had all been classmates at St John's School. There had been much talk about them all volunteering together, and the newspapers were always urging the young men to play their part and sign up. After much thought Monty joined together with Ted, Sid, Jack and the other donkey boys standing in line at the East Kent Buffs Barracks in Canterbury.

Bunty promised Monty that she would wait for him to return as they all thought that the war would be over in a few months. There would be no more ballroom dancing or competitions until her dancing partner returned safely to Margate. She promised to hang up her dancing shoes and wait it out. The heart shaped music box reigned majestically on her kidney shaped dressing table with its brush, comb and mirror set and her bottle of expensive French perfume that her older brother had brought back from a business trip to Paris before the war.

Now it was 1915 and Bunty was growing impatient. Occasionally she would wind up the music box and play the *Swan Lake* tune. She would slip on her pink ballet shoes, tie the silk ribbons and flit around her large bedroom overlooking the sea and think about Monty and her brothers. Dancing satisfied her fidgety feet and her restless desire to always be on the move. Bunty was the youngest of seven and had always been the apple of her father's eye. All her siblings had left home, some of them had married and her four brothers had all recently gone to France. They were now at the Western Front with the other Margate Lads. Bunty inherited the large bedroom that her four brothers had once shared, and there was plenty of room for her to flit around.

Monty had packed his beautiful cherry fountain pen case with the inlaid image of the swan and would regularly write to Bunty. The pen case always reminded him of his perfect dancing partner, the dreams that they both shared and his beloved home. Bunty carefully kept all of his letters in her dressing table drawer; she was beginning to accumulate a large bundle. Monty missed everyone; he was sick and tired of the war, there were no signs of peace and he absolutely hated trench life and the uncertainty of his time on earth. One day he sensed that something had happened. He and Bunty were so close but he knew deep in his heart that all was not well. He anxiously gripped his swan fountain pen case. A week later he discovered that he had a nasty case of trench foot, the rain, mud and appalling living conditions, together with a dampening of his spirits, had all played their part.

Of course Bunty still wrote but her impatience and desire to dance had drawn her to the Winter Gardens one evening with some of the young chambermaids from the Metropole Hotel who had encouraged her to join them. Now this became a regular outing. Bunty sheepishly brought her ballroom dancing shoes out of the wardrobe and was enjoying the company of young men on the dance floor. Monty had been gone from Margate for almost a year. She was lonely and waiting was so very hard for her itchy feet. "No harm," she muttered to herself, "after all I'm only dancing." The tone of Bunty's letters began to change and Monty knew, reading between the lines, that things were different. It was a set back for him and his spirits were particularly low.

The battle of Loos took place between 25 September and 13 October; it was the French and British Army offensive on the Western Front called, "The Big Push." The intention was to strike a major decisive blow and break through the enemy lines before the cold winter weather set in. Casualties on the first day were the worst yet suffered in a single day by the British Army and included 8, 500 dead. In total the battle resulted in casualties of more than 50,000 of whom some 16,000 lost their lives. Inexperienced wartime volunteers formed many British army battalions and their supporting artillery was short of heavy guns and shells. The

Battle of Loos was also the first time that the British Army used poison gas.

Monty was one of the fallen on that first day, September 25, 1915, the gunfire had been heavy and he had been badly shot in his legs, he was riddled with shrapnel. With the huge loss of life that fateful day and the horrendous injuries suffered by the badly wounded many young men had no chance at all and were left to die alone on the battlefield. Monty was one of the very lucky ones, Sid one of the Margate donkey boys, was extremely close by on that awful day. Sid had seen his good friend fall and had gone to his aid, but in doing so he had risked his own life. Sid was a strong burly lad and he managed to drag Monty back to a safer place, out of the range of the gunfire, where he could dress some of his wounds. In the chaos of the battle Sid could see that there were no stretcher-bearers or ambulances to help his friend and everything fell upon his shoulders. He dragged Monty further back to where some of the donkeys were tied up. With a great deal of effort he managed to eventually strap Monty onto one of the donkeys and lead him several miles back to a Casualty Clearing Station. Sid could see that Monty was in a very bad way by the time he reached the station. He was unconscious and had lost a lot of blood. The doctors and nursing staff didn't hold up much hope for him but they noticed that the shattered remains of a wooden pen box stuffed in his trouser pocket had stopped a bullet from severing the femoral artery in his right leg and he was in with a very slim chance.

Sid was absolutely exhausted, and collapsed on the grass outside the Casualty Clearing Station next to his donkey. He looked to the heavens above in thankfulness. He wondered just how he had managed to get his friend to safety and in with a fighting chance. He felt that somehow he must have acquired some super human strength that day; he looked lovingly over at his donkey and reflected how the donkeys had always been his faithful friends. Suddenly Sid remembered the little gold brooch with the seed pearl eye that Lord Avebury had presented him with. Ted, Sid and Jack had all worn their brooches with pride and viewed them as some kind of talisman. When they had all signed up together they decided to continue to wear their brooches under their uniforms pinned out of sight onto their vests. The brooch felt good, connecting him with his friends, his donkeys and his home in Old Town Margate. "By all accounts I should be dead," Sid whispered to his donkey, "all that gunfire and bombing, I turned back to save my friend and I just don't know how I came out of it alive and how I physically got Monty to the Clearing Station." He reached inside his jacket, unbuttoned his shirt and gently ran his large, bloodied fingers over his little gold donkey brooch with the seed pearl eye. The big burly man, no longer a boy, wondered if he had a special kind of angel watching his back on September 25th, 1915.

Dr. E. Petrie Hoyle crossed over to Ostend in Belgium on September 04, 1914 with the Army Medical Corps; in fact he was the first American doctor at the front. He went onto work in Antwerp, Malines and Fumes and in 1915 he was appointed head of Hopital Auxilliaire No.50 in Rubelles. Despite the terrible septic wounds that Dr. Hoyle worked with he had never seen a case of tetanus or gangrene develop under his care. He attributed it to his working knowledge and experience of homoeopathy. Dr. Hoyle used diluted solutions of Calendula, better known as pot or garden marigold, he poured it over compound fractures and into the large gaping holes or torn flesh of the young men brought into his care. Many of the wounds he treated were black; soldiers would arrive at his hospital from the front that had no dressings on their wounds, sometimes they had been on the road for four days. He witnessed flesh that was not only black but extremely foul smelling, the rank odour of death. Despite such desperate cases the Calendula solution helped to heal and prevented a worsening prognosis. Young doctors, supervised by Dr. Hoyle, took notice of his methods and it was under such a young doctor that Monty had the good fortune to find himself when he was brought into The Casualty Clearing Station behind the lines at Loos.

Sid's quick first aid action on the battlefield with his own supply of bandages had been of help but things took on a more favourable turn once the Calendula treatment began. Monty was eventually transferred to a French hospital where he spent several months. As Christmas approached there was talk of him finally being transferred home to Margate.

Sid wrote to Bunty to tell her all about what had happened at Loos. Bunty suspected something was wrong when she opened her music box on September 25th and had tried to turn the key. It seemed stuck and there was no music that day or from that day onwards. She began to think that she was to blame after all she had broken her promise to Monty. When the letter arrived from Sid she cried all night and decided to put her dancing shoes back in the wardrobe. There would be no more dancing until Monty could step onto the dance floor with her.

When Monty arrived home he was in a sorry state. He still had both legs but they weren't so good. He could hardly walk, each step was unbearably painful and his disposition had become gloomy and very fearful for his future. Bunty tried the best she could to cheer him up and Mr Perkins gave him back his office job sorting out his bathing machine and furniture removal accounts but life just wasn't the same for Monty. It had all lost its lustre.

Bunty spent much of her time working the reception desk at The Metropole Hotel. So many of the Margate men had now left the town and joined up, women stepped up and filled their shoes. Monty's poor health and outlook concerned her and she would occasionally pull out her handkerchief and have a good cry when she thought that no one was watching. Unknown to Bunty a roly-poly old lady, her face wizened by age, was watching her very carefully.

Bunty had noticed the old lady taking tea in the hotel foyer for the past few days, yet she had never seen her before and didn't know if she was a guest. She seemed to like the chocolate cake. Today, when she had finished her tea, she approached Bunty and gently took her hand. Looking deep into her eyes she said, "My dear go every day down to the seashore and bring back the seaweed, mind it's fresh and be sure to collect it new every day. Wrap his legs with the seaweed and leave it to soak in for a few hours. In two or three weeks you will begin to see a difference. He will dance again but you have to have faith for both of you." Bunty was about to open her mouth when a large lady with a big hat swept up to the reception desk and demanded to know why her room wasn't ready. Bunty didn't notice the wizened old lady leave but when she snatched a glance over the shoulder of the large lady she couldn't see her any more. It was as if she had faded into the ether.

Bunty really didn't know what to think, "What a very strange lady," she muttered to herself. Nevertheless something nagged at her and she felt moved to learn a little more. On her way home she stopped at Evans Chemist and Druggist shop in Margate High Street and asked them if they knew anything about seaweed. Mr Robertson peered over his horn-rimmed spectacles and reached for a rather large, dusty book high up on the shelf. Bunty shuffled from foot to foot as she tried her hardest to wait patiently for him to finish reading. He eventually found a whole section on seaweed and told Bunty that it was full of good things conducive to health, minerals such as iodine, selenium, magnesium, calcium, copper, potassium, zinc and iron. Bunty had never heard of such things but took him at his word. Everyone knew Mr Robertson, and he was well respected in the town. Apparently a seaweed bath could help relieve skin and circulation problems, detoxification, muscle aches and pains including joint stiffness. He mentioned a lot of big words that she had never heard before but she decided that tomorrow she would venture down to Margate sands and would give it a try.

As she was about to leave the shop he asked that she wait a minute. He went into the back room and came back a few minutes later with a small glass bottle. "It's for young Monty, this may also help his bad legs. This is a homoeopathic medicine called Silica we fondly call it *the homoeopathic surgeon.* It helps to bring things to the surface like splinters and bits of metal. Tell Monty to take one pill daily for several weeks. Its slow acting so please do be patient." When Bunty offered payment he waved her out the door, "It's the least I can do for a man who stepped up, volunteered and put his life on the line," he called out as the door was closing.

Instead of heading home Bunty walked along the seafront towards Margate Station. Monty had moved in with his Granny, in a two up and two down in a street of terraced homes near Margate Station and The

Royal Sea Bathing Hospital. Monty came from a large family and there wasn't room for him at home in Old Town, at least it wasn't suitable for someone who had become an invalid. The family decided that he would be more comfortable living with Granny.

Bunty excitedly explained everything that she had learnt from the curious old lady and from Evans Chemist and Druggist Store. She handed him the bottle of Silica and told him she would gather seaweed each day and bring it to Granny's home ready for him to do the wraps every evening when he returned home from work. Granny looked up from her sewing with a look of disbelief followed by amusement. Bunty wasn't at all sure if what she had shared would work and it seemed that an enormous amount of effort and patience would be required, she didn't know if she was up to it. Bunty knew that she lived in the fast lane, she wanted immediate results, and patience was clearly not a gift that she possessed. She rose up to leave she was so very weary. However, as she moved towards the door the image of the wizened old lady flashed before her eyes and her kind but stern words rang in her ear, "He will dance again but you have to have faith for both of you."

That night Bunty's sleep was particularly restless. The old lady came to her once again in a dream. Bunty saw her gathering seaweed out on the rocks in Westbrook Bay; she had filled a large wicker basket and turned to Bunty who was standing on the sands just off the Nayland Rock. Her words boomed in Bunty's ears as if they seeped through from another dimension, "Have faith Bunty, you can and must do this." The next morning, before beginning her duties as receptionist, Bunty went to see the manager at The Metropole Hotel and asked if she could switch her work duties from the usual 9am to 5pm and now work from noon until 8pm. She explained that she needed the morning hours to help a sick soldier. The manager could hardly turn down such a request; he knew Monty and so many other young Margate lads who had returned home with terrible injuries. He also knew that life would never be the same for them.

From the next day onwards Bunty left her home early each morning just as the sun was coming up, She ventured out warmly clad and wrapped up against the biting wind and icy cold. It was February 1916 and the Margate sands were always deserted. Bunty cut a very curious, windswept figure as she clambered gingerly over the slippery rocks at Westbrook Bay gathering large fronds of seaweed into two large wicker baskets. It took her an hour to harvest enough to fill her baskets and make her way to Granny's home. A large tin bath sat by the fire in the little kitchen and Bunty would fill the bath with seaweed and some water then she carefully covered it all with linen cloths waiting for Monty's return from work. Granny wasn't too keen on the smell but she could see that Bunty was dedicated and faithful and learnt to hold her nose when the smell was too bad. Some days Bunty chided herself and wondered if she was crazy because it certainly looked that way to observers walking their dogs along the seashore, especially when it was pouring with rain. Many times her long skirts and ankle boots would be soaked through, and on those days she had to quickly go home and change before making her way to the Metropole and her noon shift at the reception desk.

At first it all seemed somewhat of a farce, Monty didn't know what to think but he felt he should at least give it a try since Bunty seemed so dedicated. The laughing and snide remarks eventually stopped when Monty began to show signs of improvement. Every evening, after supper, he would sit for a couple of hours in the kitchen reading the newspaper with his feet and legs soaking in the warm water that Granny had boiled up on the stove. His injured legs were wrapped in the seaweed that Bunty had carefully harvested every morning when she had the chance. Of course she came to realize that the tides were a big problem because when it was an early morning high tide the seaweed was submerged.

Bunty knew that she couldn't take any more time off work to go out on the rocks later in the day so she paid a visit to the donkey stables up by St John's Church. There were no donkey rides on Margate beach during the winter months but a couple of the boys were always up at the stables caring for them. Bunty asked the boys if they would gather seaweed for her during the afternoons when she wasn't able to. They were quick to make a joke of it all but many of the young donkey boys knew of Ted, Sid and Jack, and could sense Bunty's urgency so finally agreed to oblige and help Monty. Subsequently Bunty and the donkey boys kept Granny and Monty generously supplied with Margate's finest and freshest seaweed.

After several weeks Monty noticed he felt stronger, healthier, much less depressed. One day his legs began to ooze alarming thick yellow pus the colour of honey. Granny went to the chemists and bought a supply of bandages so he could cover up and continue to work. After six weeks bits of wood and metal could be seen just under the surface of his skin and as time went on they could be picked out with Granny's large tweezers. It was all so fascinating to watch and Bunty together with her little band of donkey boys faithfully continued to harvest the seaweed in all kinds of weather and drop it off at Granny's home. Mr Robertson at Evans Chemist and Druggist eventually gave Granny a small bottle of homoeopathic medicine called Calc Sulph, telling Granny that the oozing had gone on for too long and this would help to sort things out. After several weeks there were no more splinters, bits of metal or pus and Monty discovered that he could walk without a stick. His legs didn't hurt anymore, his sleep was good and all his bad dreams about war and death had gone away. In the end it was the love, patience and dedication of several people that eventually reaped the most wonderful healing rewards for young Monty.

Bunty returned to her usual hours working as a receptionist at The Metropole Hotel. May was approaching and with it the summer season, the donkey boys were getting ready for a busy season on the beach and Monty felt for the first time that he and Bunty might attend a dance at The Winter Gardens. Bunty had been so busy with the seaweed that she had quite forgotten about the heart shaped music box on her dresser with the two swans set upon a pond of inlaid mother of pearl. As she pulled out her dancing shoes from the wardrobe she decided to try and turn the key. She recalled how the last time she had tried the key it had been September 25th and the first day of the battle at Loos. This was the day that Monty's legs were shattered and the day that no matter how hard she tried the key just wouldn't turn. The passage of time and nature's healing gifts brought flow and balance to Monty and Bunty's lives. Tonight the key did turn and quite easily. The gentle notes of *Swan Lake* began to fill Bunty's bedroom. She knew they had a future, she knew her faith and resolve had brought them both through a most difficult time. She had acquired the gift of patience and as she opened her door she could have sworn that she saw the smiling image of a wizened old lady in her dressing table mirror!

It was September 05, 1925 and a happy band of friends stood on Margate seashore waving to the new Margate lifeboat, *The Lord Southborough* as she motored along the seashore. Lady Southborough had just completed the launching ceremony. Ted, Sid and Jack, accompanied by their wives, together with Bunty and Monty all continued to celebrate by eating jellied eels on the seafront, washed down with a glass of port at The Benjamin Beale public house. It was a good day for Margate and its people. The happy band of friends knew all the fishermen and the lifeboat men; The Great War was a distant memory now. Ted was gainfully employed as an electrician, Sid had taken up an apprenticeship with a carpenter and Jack was a plumber. Bunty and Monty were particularly excited, as they had just taken a lease on a building and there was animated talk of their plans to establish a dancing school and their forthcoming wedding at St John's Church. Ted and Sid had made arrangements for a decorated donkey cart to take the bride to the church and then both of them to the reception. Monty's legs were never good enough to compete but he could dance and he could teach and he had the love and dedication of Bunty. It was more than enough.

As he grew older Sid spent some of his twilight years up at the donkey stables with Ted sitting on a hay bale and reminiscing. When Sid passed away his younger sister, Gladys, inherited his little gold brooch with the seed pearl eye. Sid's wife, children and other siblings had his house and the money in his bank account but Gladys had his donkey. She pinned the brooch to her tweed coat and wore it around the town with pride. As the years passed she lost count of the many people who stopped her and commented upon the little gold brooch. Gladys would tell them that it had belonged to her brother Sid, a brave soldier, a fine carpenter but best of all he had been a donkey boy. He loved his donkeys and they loved him. Gladys knew she had a treasure much more valuable than the gold from which it was crafted. She knew and really appreciated its story.

When Poppy opened her eyes, Madam was standing next to her and the little heart shaped music box with the two glass swans had dropped into Poppy's lap. "I think it belongs up on the shelf with Ted's donkey brooch, after all they are family," whispered Madam in Poppy's ear. Poppy immediately remembered the roly-poly old lady who had appeared to Bunty. She looked up again at Madam and knew in her heart that it was she. Over a hundred years had passed since the Battle of Loos. That night, lying awake in bed, Poppy toyed with the idea that Madam Popoff might be a time traveller. Of course that's the stuff of fiction, or is it?

As she began to drift off to sleep Poppy began to think again about Dr. Edward Bach and his little tattered booklet, *"The Twelve Healers."* She realized that *Impatiens* would have been a good remedy for Bunty, she was always in such a hurry and so impatient with those fidgety feet! Monty, out in the trenches, probably would have benefited from *Mimulus* for known fears and during that battle of Loos *Rock Rose.* Poppy thought about all those young soldiers going over the top, they must have been absolutely terrified. *Gentian*, for set backs, would have helped when Monty felt that things weren't the same between Bunty and himself. Also during his recovery when he was so doubtful of ever regaining his legs and getting back on the dance floor.

Chapter 21

Poppy loved Margate in the summertime, she realized that she had been in the town for almost a year and oh so much had happened in her life since she stepped off that last train on that fateful day in early July. The field of donkeys, up by the North Foreland Lighthouse, became a regular stopping off place on her morning bike rides with Jack the Lad. She always carried a generous supply of apples and carrots. Donkeys had never held much interest for her but since Ted, Sid and Monty's stories she saw them in a very different light. She also became much more aware of all the poppies, her namesake, that grew by the side of the fields and in the rock gardens as she made her way down Madeira Walk hill towards Ramsgate Harbour, Ship Shape Café, Winston and the sausages.

It was 2018 and the 100-year anniversary of The Great War. As Poppy pedalled she confessed to herself that she had never given war much thought, names on memorials and in history books had been just that, names. Working at the Madam Popoff Vintage Emporium had truly opened her eyes. Poppy had become privy to the lives of many people. She had felt their joys and their sorrows, life's hardships and the times of celebration. Poppy saw that it was love, friendship, gratitude and forgiveness that kept the wheels of life and fortune well oiled and turning.

Today she made a point of stopping off at the Margate War Memorial in Trinity Gardens and thanking the names etched in the stone because now they had faces, stories, hopes and dreams. She thanked them for their ultimate sacrifice. From the stories that had come to light Poppy really felt these men were no longer anonymous, she felt that she knew them like a brother and for the first time she fully comprehended and understood the absolute tragedy and waste that war brings in its wake.

There were 457 names on The Great War Memorial. Later, when she visited the Margate Museum, she learnt that 429 of those names had been servicemen, 18 were victims of enemy air raids on the town and 10 were munitions workers who were killed as a result of an explosion at The Faversham Lees Explosive Factory on Sunday April 02, 1916. She also learnt that there had been 38 air raids on Margate during the Great War and many schools and hotels were lent to The Red Cross and became temporary hospitals to care for the wounded returning on the ambulance trains to Margate from the Western Front. There had been so many refugees pouring in from Belgium that a relief committee was formed and Margate people had taken them in and helped the best that they could. A large home for Belgium refugees was opened in Westbrook.

As Poppy sat down by The Great War Memorial she opened her backpack and pulled out the little tattered booklet by Dr. Edward Bach, *"The Twelve Healers."* Poppy read once again *Mimulus* for known fears, *Rock Rose* for terror, *Clematis* for those who are in some way unconscious and *Gentian* for those who are easily discouraged. Poppy reflected how all of these helpers from nature would be helpful in today's world and most useful all those years back in the trenches and in the aftermath of such devastation.

It was nearly the end of June, a very hot day and the beach was crowded. Cycling along Margate seafront reminded Poppy of Bunty and the seaweed. Over the past year she had seen some adverts for a newly established company with a shop up on Cliff Terrace called Haeckels. Apparently they gathered and used Margate seaweed for a line of skin and beauty potions and lotions. Poppy smiled and pictured Monty sitting by Granny's fire wrapped in Margate seaweed, she marvelled at all the things that nature puts at our disposal for our health and healing.

Poppy certainly wasn't expecting to see a beautiful silver fox fur stole tucked away in a small box that had been left on the doorstep when she had opened up that day. It was unusual to see furs in Madam Popoff's shop and if they were there they were always fake, never the real thing. Later Poppy sat down with a glass of lemonade. It had been a busy day and it was near closing time. The shop was now empty. She gingerly fingered the stole and gently stroked the head and paws of the fox and drifted back to another time.

Clara was gainfully employed on the shop floor at Bobby & Co located on the corner of Margate High Street and Queen Street. She was sweet but rather a wobbly young girl. She came from a large family and her mother would always scold her and say, "Clara, money doesn't grow on trees, if you want nice things you'll have to go and work for them." Clara had worked at Bobby's since she was 16. She liked clothes, make up and all the latest hair fashions. Bobby's suited her. It was a large and very respectable establishment. All the wealthy ladies who lived in Margate and the surrounding areas would shop there and during the holiday season it was busy with well-heeled visitors staying in the town. Clara had begun her career in the stocking, glove and hat department but when she turned 18 she was promoted; which meant extra wages and a trusted position in the high-end costumes and fur department.

Clara absolutely loved the feel of the expensive fur coats, wraps and stoles. She would carefully examine the heads and paws of the fox and mink stoles and would stroke them when no one was looking. Exotic things easily turned Clara's head; she didn't really look beyond their face value. She certainly didn't think about the poor animals whose lives had been sacrificed in the name of fashion. Furs in the 1930's were high fashion and all the classy ladies wore them. Clara was a girl who was easily led. She lacked confidence and found it difficult to make up her mind, looking to others for advice and leadership and avoiding all confrontation. When she saw her good friend Matilda with her hands in the till she didn't know what to do. She knew that stealing was wrong but Matilda was her friend. Clara toyed with the idea that if she told on her friend then she may never talk to her again, so Clara learned to navigate her way through life by turning a blind eye. It wasn't always a wise choice and it happened a lot, it meant that she didn't have to think for herself too much.

Clara was drawn to the glitzy things in life, nice dresses, parties and dances at the Winter Gardens and Dreamland Ballroom. Best of all she liked to wander down to S.H. Cuttings in the Old Town and browse their windows during her lunch break. The windows were filled with sparkly gems, rubies, emeralds, sapphires, diamonds, gold watches and bracelets. Clara was drawn in by the glamour, wealth and prestige of such things. When Enrico came along she was easily charmed. He came from an Italian family who had immigrated to Margate a generation ago seeking a better life. He was tall, debonair, smartly dressed; quite the dandy and he even had an exotic name but in truth his slick brylcreem pomaded hair matched his slick and devious personality.

Enrico liked his name, which meant homeowner or king. He had decided from a very early age that he would be a king in Margate. As he grew up his friends knew him as the, "wide boy of the town." Enrico liked to wheel and deal. He had his fingers in a lot of pies most of them muddy and decidedly shady, he frequented the billiard halls and back room gambling joints where a lot more than drinking and smoking took place. They were dens of nefarious activity. The thing that pleased him most was having a glamorous woman attached to his arm. He met the attractive, vulnerable Clara at the Dreamland Ballroom on New Year's Eve 1933.

Enrico immediately knew that he had a good catch, a pretty young thing that would bend to his every whim. He began to wine and dine the impressionable Clara and when they became engaged he presented her with a large diamond ring from S.H. Cuttings and a beautiful silver fox stole purchased from Bobby & Co. It was a special order shipped in all the way from Wisconsin in America. However, the wedding plans were hastily brought forward when Clara found herself pregnant. Enrico wasn't too happy hearing this news. She gave up her job at Bobby & Co and a very swift register office marriage was arranged.

It was only a few weeks after their wedding that Clara lost the child. Things took an alarming down turn as soon as the gold band gripped Clara's delicate finger. Enrico's shady side raised its ugly face. He began to return home very late at night after he had been drinking and gambling. Clara lay awake in bed waiting for him, she was lonely, missed her friends and all the nice genteel ladies whom she had assisted over the years at

Bobby & Co. They had set up home in a rented house on Fort Crescent across from the Winter Gardens, in a very nice, affluent neighbourhood but Clara didn't realize that Enrico was hard pressed to find the rent. His fingers continued to dabble in questionable wheeling and dealing activities and after the wedding he began to venture into the even darker world of drugs.

Very late one night, as he came to bed, Clara plucked up the courage to question his nocturnal movements. He suddenly turned upon her; with a swift lash of his arm he threw her across the room and then kicked her many times in the stomach with intent to kill their unborn child. Her eye was blackened and badly cut above the left eyebrow as she struck the sharp corner of a cabinet. Clara was in total shock; badly bruised and immediately sensing something was wrong with the baby. Enrico continued to rant and rage like a wild animal. Clara was terrified, as she had never witnessed such a monster before. She feared for her life and knew that she had to get out, so mustering all of her courage and energy she rushed downstairs towards the front door. There was no time to put on a jacket or shoes; she knew that she just had to run. Thankfully it was late summer and the air was warm. It was long past midnight and the street was deserted but well lit by a full moon. As she looked over her shoulder she could see Enrico reaching for his shoes and holding a large kitchen carving knife in his hand readying himself to chase her down the street.

It was the sight of an old lady standing in the middle of the street by the Winter Gardens that stopped him in his tracks. She was roly-poly and had a wizened face but she firmly stood her ground and Enrico knew that she would be a formidable witness; she raised her right hand as one might signal the intention to STOP. At that moment Enrico felt a bolt of lightning shoot through his body. It was so intense that he dropped the knife and so painful that he yelled out very loudly in anguish. The loud commotion woke the neighbours, lights turned on in the bedrooms and some people hastily spilled onto the street. Enrico retreated inside and shut the door.

Clara collapsed in her lily-white nightgown onto the street sobbing, shaking, badly cut and bruised. She was in obvious pain and trauma. There were many broken pieces that needed fixing. Two elderly spinsters agreed to take her into their home, kind ladies who had once been nursing sisters during The Great War. They helped Clara into a warm bed, cleaned her up and plied her with warm tea laced with brandy and called the doctor. No one noticed the old lady slip quietly into the night.

Clara was extremely traumatized, the doctor came quickly and gave her some medicine to calm her down, he sat with her throughout the night as labour pains had begun and early the next morning she delivered a stillborn baby girl. Fanny and Ethel did the best they could to make her comfortable. They cleaned her deep cut above the eye with Calendula solution, soothed her bruises with Arnica ointment and held her hand. A few days had passed since the terrible incident and they were becoming increasingly concerned for her wellbeing as she kept slipping into some kind of comatose state. Occasionally she would wake up, look around the room in terror. She didn't seem to recognize anyone and she would scream out, then would sink back down into the bed and once again faded away into oblivion. The spinsters sent for the doctor again but he didn't know what to do. The uterine bleeding had stopped but she was in a bad way. He could only offer more of the calming medicine that he had given the first night but that prescription produced no results.

As time marched on Fanny decided to consult with one of the chemists in the town, knowing that he kept supplies of homoeopathic medicines in his back room. Fanny became familiar with homoeopathy when she had worked as a nursing sister at one of the hospitals on the Western Front. The chemist patiently listened to Fanny's account of all that had happened and consulted with another colleague in the shop. Eventually he retired to the back room and emerged some time later with a tiny packet of pills and gave his instructions to Fanny. "This is homoeopathic Opium, we use this remedy when someone has experienced a very bad fright and they have never recovered from the ordeal, it's as if they remain in the frightened state. It is indicated for coma and periods of wakefulness where the nerves are really on edge. Please give her just one single dose two tiny pills dissolved in a little water then watch and wait. I believe that she will recover within a few days."

"Magic pills," beamed Ethel as Clara who sat propped up in bed, was pale but lucid. The Opium had restored her equilibrium. Eventually the bruising faded, the skin above her left eyebrow healed and following the loving care and attention given by Fanny and Ethel she was ready to face the world again. Clara had never had a good mentor in her life. She came from a large family where her mother and father were always working or preoccupied with household chores, and there was never any time left to give her the attention or guidance that she so badly needed. Clara had fallen into some bad company when she began working on the shop floor at Bobby & Co. She was easily led and misguided. There had been no one to take her aside and teach her some pearls of wisdom. Clara's pearls were the bright shiny jewels on display in S.H. Cutting's windows.

Fanny and Ethel saw to it that she was given a lot of loving guidance. She stayed with them for the next four months physically recovering but also growing stronger in her mind and spirit. Clara grew comfortably into her own person, she began to learn the art of discernment, how to speak up when things weren't right, how to choose wisely the company that she kept and how to firmly make her own wise decisions, ones that would feed her spirit. Clara changed before their eyes; she was no longer the helpless little fledgling that had fallen from the nest. With the love that she received from Fanny and Ethel, Clara was ready to soar.

After Christmas 1933 she began a new journey. Fanny and Ethel had told her many stories about their own nursing careers. Clara appreciated their love and dedication; she felt that she couldn't return to the shop floor at Bobby & Co, her life was ready to head off in a different direction. She made up her mind to become a nurse and enrolled at The Royal Sea Bathing Hospital. She received instructions to report for duty on January 02, 1934. Clara was offered accommodation in the nurse's home, a pleasant place a stone's throw from the hospital and the sea, built in 1922. This would be her new beginning, a second chance at life.

The divorce came through very quickly as there had been plenty of witnesses that awful night in the late summer. Several neighbouring men swore that they had seen Enrico standing in the doorway brandishing a knife, the doctor's detailed report confirmed the violence that Clara had suffered. The court didn't take too kindly to a man who had attempted to murder a woman and her unborn child. Clara was free.

It was a bitterly cold day on January 01, 1934 when Ethel and Fanny accompanied Clara to the nurses' home in Westbrook and helped her to move in. As Clara peered down from her second floor bedroom window and waved them goodbye she caught a glimpse of another woman standing with them, a stranger, roly-poly, with a deeply wrinkled face and a wonderful smile. The old lady blew Clara a kiss.

Clara went on to become a Queen Alexandra's Royal Army Nursing Sister during World War 2. She served in many military hospitals in Britain and overseas and eventually married an army captain at the end of the war. She never forgot Fanny and Ethel and endeavoured to repay their love in all that she did. When Clara eventually retired she helped to establish a home for battered women. It was a life well lived.

Poppy looked down at the gorgeous silver fox stole, which she knew belonged to a different time, a dark time in Clara's life, and she realized it wasn't welcome in Madam's shop. Furs are taboo in this day and age, as people have generally become much more concerned about the rights of animals and wearing a real fur coat in the 21st century can bring the owner nothing but trouble. Poppy set it aside for Madam's allotment bonfire. She reflected upon Clara's life and how it had been so transformed by the deep love and care of two elderly ladies, who had set her upon the right path in life and been a beacon of light in her darkest days. Poppy reached for her copy of *"The Twelve Healers,"* by Edward Bach and reread *Rock Rose* for terror. Clara must surely have needed this remedy when she ran for her life that fateful night in the summer of 1933. When she fell into a coma after delivering her still born child *Clematis* for dreamy, unconscious states would have been helpful and when she was such a naive girl working at Bobby's, easily led, influenced and misguided by others *Cerato* may have prevented such painful life lessons. *Cerato* is the remedy for those who don't have enough confidence in themselves to make their own decisions.

Poppy shut up the shop and before she ventured home to Lookout Retreat she cycled along the seafront towards the Royal Sea Bathing Hospital. She passed the lone lifeboat man gazing out to the sea and the forever Christmas house. Poppy propped her bicycle up against the wall of the old nurses' home. It had been converted into luxury flats, a Grade 2 listing having kept it from the hands of the demolition squad. Poppy gazed up and wondered which window had been Clara's bedroom. She began to ask herself why her name kept on appearing in the stories that she had become privy to. After all wasn't Opium made from the Poppy?

Chapter 22

July arrived and Poppy's first year anniversary, marking her relocation to Margate, was imminent. Madam suggested earlier on in the year that Poppy might consider taking some time off in the summer. Isadora had neighbours who were twins, bright young girls who were looking forward to taking up a place at university in the autumn; apparently they approached Madam and asked if she could give them a job over the summer. The twins were set to begin work in a couple of weeks. Poppy acted upon Madam's suggestion and made arrangements to spend some time with an old friend from London. They arranged a hiking holiday in Switzerland and Austria and then some time together in Italy. Poppy was looking forward to a long break and returning to Margate near the end of August. Madam hinted that lots of new things were on the horizon, business was booming, the shop had done really well since Poppy crossed the threshold just under a year ago. Madam's hunting expeditions were now focused upon other properties. There was talk about the possibility of opening up a satellite vintage costume emporium in nearby Ramsgate or Broadstairs later in the year.

It was Poppy's last day, Monday July 9th; she was exhausted, the shop had been unusually busy over the past few days and she was really looking forward to her trip to Europe. She arrived much earlier than usual to finish some extra cleaning and ensure that everything was in order before the twins and Isadora took over. A black plastic bin liner had been left on the doorstep overnight with a hastily scribbled note asking Madam to sort through and use what she could. The note ended with a curious phrase that immediately caught Poppy's attention, *"from a grateful admirer of all that you do, I'm one of your special people."* It took Poppy back to last summer when she first paid a visit to the Madam Popoff Vintage Emporium and had seen the small note in the window as she was leaving, *"extra help needed, only special people need apply."* Poppy recalled how angry she had felt when she had seen that note. However, things had taken a much more positive turn in Poppy's life since that fateful day. She felt a lot more confident; she had learnt so much about being human and life's mysteries. She had begun to understand the importance of a healthy mind and more than anything else she had witnessed the amazing things that happen when love, gratitude and forgiveness steer one's ship. Poppy knew that she had Madam Popoff to thank along with the love of Aunt Flora who had given her a home in Margate and a little tattered booklet called, *"The Twelve Healers,"* written by a man who had passed away 82 years ago! Poppy knew that Edward Bach had begun to grace her with his presence in her life every single day, encouraging her to step up and don the mantle of a healer.

Poppy was eager to finish up her chores and sit down with a cup of coffee. As she heard the clock on Margate Clock Tower strike 9.30am she was ready to take a break and sift through the dustbin liner. There really wasn't much to look through, a few psychedelic print dresses from the 1960's, a garish pink handbag and matching shoes from the same era. However, as she reached the bottom of the bin liner she pulled out an old record album by the Beatles, *"Please, Please Me - with Love Me Do and 12 other songs."* It appeared to be an early version from the UK's Parlophone label; it had a black and gold label on the vinyl and songs credited to Dick James Music Company. Growing up Poppy had really loved the Beatles; even today she still loved to hear their songs and was planning to visit the Winter Gardens in November when a Beatles tribute band would be playing. She lightly ran her hand across the album's colourful cover and held it close to her heart and yet again Poppy was transported back to another time.

The 1963 calendar on Jane's dorm wall at The Royal School for Deaf Children had a big red circle around the dates July 8 – 13. Jane was particularly excited. Britain's fabulous disc stars; *The Beatles* were scheduled to play in Margate at The Winter Gardens up on Fort Crescent. *Billy. J. Kramer with the Dakotas* would be a supporting band. Jane had been following their fortunes for some time and just like any other normal fifteen year old in 1963 she was crazy about boys, trendy clothes, pop music and disco dancing. There was only one problem with Jane and it was major, she was deaf.

Jane's mother didn't realize that she had contracted German measles back in 1947 when she was in her early pregnancy with her third child. She was a busy mother and already had two lively young children to care for. She thought that her low-grade fever, headache, runny nose and pink eye were a touch of the flu or a cold. The mild rash, which started on her face and crept down her body, came and went quickly and she didn't think anything of it. When baby Jane failed to meet the usual milestones that her other young children had reached, the health visitor seemed concerned and following a barrage of tests the worst was confirmed, Jane was pronounced profoundly deaf. Her mother had contracted German measles in her pregnancy. Naturally her loving parents were devastated and did all they could to help Jane in her early years. Any extra household income was spent on a private teacher for Jane who taught her sign language.

Jane stayed at home until she was 11 years old but at that time the family decided that she would benefit more from a boarding school education at the highly respected Royal School for Deaf Children in Margate. It was a difficult decision but everyone felt that she would benefit from specialist help and teaching. Jane was a bright girl who could read and write but being totally deaf was a profound handicap. She didn't speak either and the neighbourhood kids weren't nice, calling her all kinds of names and chiding her. Jane's sister and brother would try and stand up for her. Her brother often came home with a black eye; having been in so many fights defending his little sister. Being labelled, "deaf and dumb" was a major social stigma. Those who didn't know Jane also thought she was probably an imbecile and consequently treated her badly and with little respect.

Actually, Jane was quite relieved when her mother and older sister accompanied her on the long train ride to Margate. It took them the better part of a day; they were going to help her settle in for the beginning of the September term, 1959. She was finally leaving the neighbourhood bullies behind and embarking upon her very own new adventure. Her mother assured her that she would make friends easily. After all everyone was in the same boat, all the students had major hearing problems just like Jane, for once she would be amongst her own tribe.

On their long train journey to Margate Jane's mother helped her to read the pamphlet explaining how the school came into existence and their teaching methods.

"The Royal School for Deaf Children was founded in 1792 when the evangelical minister reverend Townsend of Bermondsey began to raise funds; it was the first public institution to provide free education for the deaf, a wonderful development in a time when deaf and disabled people without a considerable private income had very difficult lives. In fact just a year prior to this Dr. John Coakley Lettsom a Quaker physician founded The Royal Sea Bathing Hospital in Margate for the poor people of London suffering from TB.

The Royal School for Deaf Children opened a branch in Margate in 1876 and it moved entirely from its base in London to Margate in 1905, so that the pupils could benefit from the clean sea air and no longer have to breathe in London's pollution. The School is situated on a large plot of land adjacent to Victoria Road in Margate; the imposing redbrick building has turrets and there is a gothic tower. By 1938, there were 418 pupils and 150 staff; children came from all over the country. After the war day pupils were admitted for the first time. Today we have a large and very caring staff and welcome your child to Margate. Please rest assured that we will help your child to be the best that they can and well prepared for a fulfilling life.

Please note that The Milan Conference of 1880 decided that the Oral Method of Teaching was superior to sign language. The Royal School for the Deaf adopted this Oral Method and it has been the basis of our teaching since 1880. We do not teach sign language and we encourage hearing parents and the family of deaf children to use the Oral Method, better known as lip reading. Sign language is not encouraged."

Life wasn't as rosy as Jane had anticipated, because she really missed her family. The Royal School for Deaf Children was a large institution and in the early months she felt lost. Her classmates were pleasant enough after all they really were all in the same boat but many of them weren't as stable as Jane. She soon realized that not everyone had the good fortune to come from a loving, caring, home where mum and dad were around to dole out advice and a big hug when needed. Jane came from a home where there was always food on the table, a clean, safe, loving place. She had always taken such things for granted, The Royal School for Deaf Children opened her eyes in many respects. Jane grew up very fast. She became street wise and avoided the troublemakers, the kids who had bad temper tantrums, those that threw things and banged their heads against the wall when they were frustrated or angry. Then there were the kids who hid under the bed or the school desks and no matter how hard the matron or the class teacher tried they just wouldn't come out. Jane had of course learnt sign language at home and became quite distressed when it really sunk in that signing wasn't acceptable. That wasn't how they did things in Margate, she would have to learn to lip read. Lip-reading caused a lot of extra stress it wasn't easy. Jane quickly became discouraged and began to isolate herself, she retreated into her own inner world, frequenting a dream world of far off places, being able to hear, lying somewhere on a pure white exotic beach under palm trees in a warm breeze without a care.

It was Cookie who eventually brought Jane back down to earth. Cookie's real name was Susan but the only time anyone called her that was if she was in big trouble and that happened a lot. Cookie was adventurous and took Jane under her wing; they had a lot of fun together. Cookie had also been taught sign language in her own home so when no one was looking this is how they communicated; it was a skill that cemented their friendship. The boys would dare each other to climb the tall gothic tower and etch their initials high up in the stonework, it was a rite of passage for newcomers. The gothic tower could not be accessed from inside the building only from the outside. Cookie taught Jane how to climb she didn't want the boys to have the upper hand. Together they eventually scaled the huge tower and carved their names side-by-side together with a little heart high up in the stonework and from then on they saw themselves as *twins in heaven.*

Cookie was particularly fortunate, as her parents and brother lived in Margate just up the road in Milton Avenue. Cookie boarded Monday through Thursday nights but she went home on Friday after school for the weekend. During their long friendship Cookie would often take Jane home for the weekend, her family lived in a small terraced house that was always warm and welcoming. Her mum loved to cook and they both overindulged in all the cupcakes, scones, iced biscuits and pies on offer. In fact everything that a young girl conscious of her figure shouldn't be eating! The two girls became inseparable. They read the same comics, fell in love with all the things that young teens in the 1960's liked to do and Cookie would come and stay at Jane's home during the long school holidays. Cookie had never been on a train journey before she met Jane. These trips were always seen as a huge adventure.

As time moved on they became more and more interested in pop music, they could both feel the vibrations and rhythm of music and enjoyed it as much as hearing people. Apparently sounds are processed in the same part of the brain for everyone whether they can hear or are hearing impaired. By 1963 everyone was talking about *The Beatles*, they were growing in popularity and were coming to Margate. The girls saved up their pocket money and planned to attend their concert at The Winter Gardens. Unfortunately when the time came for Cookie to buy the tickets she found that the only seats available were on Tuesday July 9th for the later performance. The summer holidays hadn't begun yet, the girls were still in school and Tuesday night was definitely off limits and no one was allowed off the premises. This didn't deter Cookie. She went ahead and bought the two tickets for the later performance anyway, they would not be missing *The Beatles!*

They carefully hatched their plan. Cookie purchased a nice bar of chocolate and waved it in front of Mick the gardener. She pleaded with him to leave his large wooden wheelbarrow out by the wall that evening instead of locking it away in his shed. The girls planned to use it to climb onto and then to scramble over the red brick wall into Victoria Road. Other bars of chocolate coaxed the younger girls to cover for them when matron did her dorm rounds before lights out.

It was a night to remember, thrilling and ecstatic. Their favourite tune was *Twist and Shout*. The girls danced in their seats and waved their hands just like everyone else. The young men performing on the stage captured their hearts; it was an incredibly joyous, exciting evening. The two girls were part of something they had never experienced before, a community brought together by music and some kind of magic that held them all in awe. The moon had been full on Saturday July 06th so they easily navigated their way back to Victoria Road and crept into bed, it was late and all was well with the world, Jane smiled, it felt so good to be alive.

The last week of school was uneventful; Cookie was looking forward to taking the train to Jane's home during the second week of August. They had so many holiday plans. Jane remembered Monday 05th August very clearly, the moon was particularly bright, she couldn't sleep, and she lay awake for hours and thought back to that lovely, magical evening spent with Cookie in July at Margate's Winter Gardens. As she continued to lie awake she suddenly began to feel stabs of sharp pain, firstly in her head and then in her heart. Jane knew something was terribly wrong but didn't know what. She had never had these sensations before. When Jane eventually fell into a restless sleep she dreamed of her good friend Cookie. Cookie was standing by her bed. She was very bright, that's what Jane remembered the most, she was shining and she was singing. She was actually singing a Beatles song from the concert; *I Saw Her Standing There*. Jane couldn't hear and Cookie couldn't sing but in that dream Jane knew that she had heard the song and yes, Cookie was actually singing, she was also smiling and blowing Jane a kiss. As she began to fade away Jane saw her turn and wave goodbye. Jane woke with a jolt, she was crying.

The crying didn't stop for a very long time. Jane begged her mother to call Cookie's parents in the morning after breakfast and ask if all was well, things just didn't feel right. Jane knew something bad had happened when her father came home from work at lunchtime, he never did this. The two of them sat Jane down and tried the best they could to explain what had happened. Apparently Cookie had been feeling unwell yesterday afternoon. She complained about having a terrible headache, her neck was stiff and she suddenly developed a very high fever. The doctor told her parents to take her immediately to Margate Hospital as they suspected meningitis. The condition was extremely serious and sadly Cookie passed away at 3 am this morning, apparently there was nothing the doctors could do for her.

It was such a shock and Jane was still numb with disbelief as she returned to Margate a few days later with her family. It was the saddest journey of her life. Matron was waiting for them on the station platform; having arranged a car to take the family to St John's Church for the late afternoon funeral and then onto Margate Cemetery. Jane didn't know what to think. Her whole world had fallen apart, her best friend was gone, and it wasn't ever supposed to have been like this. This wasn't their plan, there were supposed to be more Beatles concerts and they were both looking forward to their last year at school before graduating into the big wide world outside The Royal School for Deaf Children. Everyone was crying. Cookie's parents were beside themselves with grief and Jane sank into the depths of despair.

Looking back on things a few years later Jane believed that it was Cookie who must have sent the roly-poly old lady with a wizened face that burial day. Jane remembered standing by the family grave as the men lowered Cookie's small coffin into the ground. The strange old woman was standing under an oak tree near the huge lifeboat memorial to the Margate Surfboat, *Friend To All Nations.* The old woman was fixing her gaze upon Jane and holding up a small bunch of beautiful white flowers. From her lips Jane could read the words, *"Star of Bethlehem."* She was holding the bouquet up and out towards Jane. Jane didn't know what came over her but she went over to the old woman, took the bouquet, felt its calming energy and then quietly threw it into Cookie's grave. It landed with a gentle thud on top of her coffin.

The old woman visited her quite regularly; Jane couldn't work out if she was an angel. Picture books always painted angels with long white dresses and wings. This woman was roly-poly, her face was wizened and she didn't have wings. She always offered comfort to Jane in her darkest moments. She told Jane that people don't grieve if they haven't loved and that God had another plan for Cookie and it wasn't for us to ask. She told Jane that life must go on. The clocks were still ticking here on earth and Jane had important work to do. She appeared on Jane's first day back at school in September, on Cookie's birthday in October and later in life on odd occasions when Jane was feeling particularly alone and vulnerable. The old woman always called Jane, *"one of my special people."*

Jane was special; Cookie's parents gave her *The Beatles* album that they had purchased earlier in the year for their daughter's 16th birthday in October. Jane treasured it for a very long time. In time the old woman formally introduced herself as, "Madam Popoff." Jane eventually went to college and as her life continued she became an advocate for people with disabilities. She held down a good job in London and as more time passed she met a young man who was also deaf and they married. Jane would often visit Margate with her husband and young family. They always headed up to Milton Avenue and Cookie's home where there was always a warm welcome and plenty of iced buns.

When the old deaf school building was eventually dismantled and the tower was taken down workmen discovered the graffiti carved by the pupils who had once upon a time scaled the gothic tower unbeknown to the staff. It was Bert who found two names amongst the boys. The etching read, *Cookie and Jane* and a little heart was drawn between them. Construction of a new school building begun in 1972 and was completed in 1976. The Royal School for Deaf Children eventually closed its doors very suddenly in December 2015 after the John Townsend Trust, which ran it, went into administration. The Royal School for Deaf Children had operated for more than 220 years. The sudden closure left a lot of distressed staff without work and students without a school.

Sadly deaf children were often isolated from their peers because it was so difficult for them to hear and understand what went on at school and at home. Concentrating upon lip reading can be so difficult and very tiring. It's not surprising that many deaf children left school with few qualifications because they didn't fully understand what was going on, not because they had a learning disability. A report in the 1970's eventually concluded that The Oral Method had been unsuccessful and had made it more difficult for deaf children to learn. In present times sign language is considered the best method for the deaf to communicate.

Jane became heavily involved in the new movement for signing, it became her life's path and now at the grand old age of 70 it was time for her to retire and enjoy life relaxing in a small bungalow that she and her husband had purchased near the cliffs in Margate. It had been a life well lived. There were lots of things to sort through as they vacated their London home and in one bag Jane carefully placed some old dresses from the 1960's. It was also time for her to let go of her old Beatle's album, especially as everything was available on the IPod now.

Time had moved on but the passage of time had not healed the deep sorrow that Jane always felt because she had lost her *twin in heaven.* Nevertheless, Jane had been able to carry on. Her life was full of movement and grace, she still loved the Beatles and quite often, just like the song, *I Saw Her Standing There,* Jane felt that Cookie was around, standing there. She hadn't abandoned Jane, she was just in some other place offering support and encouragement whenever she could and reminding Jane to always have fun, and understand that once in a while it was ok to be a little naughty. Jane always looked fondly back on that magical evening when two young girls had hopped over the wall and made their merry way to Margate's Winter Gardens. In time Jane accepted this; it was life. People love and they lose. Jane was grateful for the little time they had been together. It was good and it had to be enough. Jane knew in her heart that in the end that was the only way to look at it.

Poppy opened her eyes, yet again she was crying. The first thing that she remembered was *The Star of Bethlehem.* She didn't know what this meant, but decided to investigate further. She quickly pulled out her phone and searched for flowers on Google. Then a sudden thought made her think about Bach remedies. Poppy was surprised to read that there were actually 38 remedies and there it was on the website bachcentre.com, *Star of Bethlehem,* Dr. Bach's remedy for shock, trauma and grief. Poppy could see this must have been a later addition to his work, *"The Twelve Healers."*

Poppy remembered the old lady and how Jane had thought that she might be an angel. Poppy looked up, Madam Popoff had put in an appearance. She was hovering over Poppy's shoulder as she exclaimed, "Poppy that album you are holding is rare, it's worth a lot of money. We'll have an auction house look at it. I think it will raise enough for a very good donation to a charity of your choice. Which charity would you like me to make arrangements to contact while you are away on vacation?" There was only one possibility. Poppy sighed and looked up, "a charity focused upon deaf people. Thank you Madam, and a very big thank you for gracing my life."

The rest of the day was busy with customers and when Poppy decided to shut up shop at 5pm she really was ready for her holiday break in Europe. It was time to return to Lookout Retreat and pack her bags. She had learnt so much and now it was time to rest and perhaps assimilate and digest as she hiked through the mountains of Europe. It had been quite the year; Poppy felt she had been blessed with a second chance at life.

Before leaving she pulled out her copy of, *"The Twelve Healers"* and began to reflect upon Jane's life. Poppy thought that *Bach Gentian* for set backs would have been a particularly helpful remedy when Jane first arrived at The Royal School for Deaf Children and discovered that sign language was not acceptable. Lip reading was so difficult it must have been a real challenge for Jane and Poppy could see how she must have easily become disheartened. Jane eventually turned inwards, lost interest in life and was clearly very unhappy with her present circumstances. Jane escaped and took herself to far off places away from school and the pressures of life. Poppy recalled how Jane would dream of white beaches, palm trees and being able to hear and thought possibly *Clematis* may have helped her at that time. Then of course there was the comfort of *Star of Bethlehem* for the shock and unhappiness of Cookie's passing.

Learning about the *"Twelve Healers"* focused Poppy's attention upon her own life. In the past she had become disheartened on many occasions and when things were very bad the strategy of taking oneself off to some far away place in the future was all so familiar. Poppy's work colleagues up in London would often chide her and tell her to ground herself and stop spending so much time in fairy land. Jane didn't have any Bach remedies to help her but she was lucky, Cookie had come into her life. Friendship is so important Poppy knew that a good friend or mentor was as good as a lifeboat. She smiled to herself and remembered planning the soirees back in the winter months. Madam had exclaimed, "We are herd animals we just have to figure out how to herd them in here!" *Bach Water Violet* also came to mind, again one of the *Twelve Healers,* for those quiet people who in health or illness like to be alone, independent people, capable and self - reliant. Poppy reflected how sometimes people can be too alone. Definitely long winter months shut up in Margate isn't good for anyone's health or morale!

Poppy was curious to learn more about the life of Edward Bach, so she picked up her phone and opened the Bach website again. Poppy read that the good doctor had been born on September 24th, 1886 in a small village outside Birmingham and passed away in 1936. He had a great love for the countryside especially Wales where his family originated and it was in Wales where he found the first of his *"Twelve Healers."* He was a compassionate man who wished to help those who were suffering, wanting to find a simple form of healing that would cure all forms of disease, one that was accessible to everyone. As a schoolboy he would dream that healing power flowed from his hand and all whom he touched would be healed. As he grew in knowledge and experience he eventually abandoned his work in conventional medicine and also the work that he had been doing as a highly respected bacteriologist and he ventured out into the countryside to find his superior healers of mankind, his remedies made from flowers and trees. He also discovered that he really did have the power of healing touch. People would be healed just by the touch of his hand. Poppy immediately thought about Madam Popoff, she recalled that over the past year Madam touched many people. She would take their hand and say, "come." Madam would sit for hours in the back room with distressed people who crossed her threshold. Poppy had watched how sometime she just talked but sometimes she simply held their hand.

Poppy looked down at her own long slender fingers and her delicate hands. Working with Madam Popoff had taught her the importance of her hands. She had learnt to feel her way through life, to discern stories and ownership just by touching the things that crossed Madam's threshold. Now she was beginning to understand the mysteries of healing. She knew in her heart that being in Margate had set her upon a path of healing, healing herself, but more than this she was learning how she might be of assistance to others in distress.

At long last she put her tattered little booklet away and looked at her watch again, it was long past 5pm. She fumbled in her bag for the large iron key to lock the door. As she reached deeper into her large carpetbag she came across an old envelope. Written on the back in very spidery handwriting was a note:

"In the end three things matter; how much you loved, how gently you lived, and how gracefully you let go of things not meant for you."

Author's Note

I have always wanted to write a book. Although I have been published in professional journals this really is a new venture for me and here at long last my vision has become a reality! I wanted to write a novel, an easy read that holidaymakers can enjoy while relaxing on a beach somewhere.

Margate is in my blood; it's the place of my birth and the place I have always been drawn back to. The famous Margate artist Tracey Emin once said, *"You can take the girl out of Margate but you can't take Margate out of the girl."*

In more recent years Margate has enjoyed an up turn in its fortunes. It is wonderful to witness the Margate that I knew in my childhood and youth returning to more prosperous times. When I visit relatives and friends every summer the beach is crowded, the cafes, pubs, shops and restaurants are busy and Margate is presently enjoying a boom in business.

I wanted to write about the little town, explore some of its history and its interesting places and people then weave all of this into a novel that a holidaymaker might enjoy. During the summer of 2018 I was wandering through Margate Old Town and I was drawn into the popular vintage clothing stores. I have always loved fashion and frocks, my mum and aunt Lillian were wonderful dressmakers and I fondly recall regular childhood jaunts up to Canterbury and the market to buy patterns and material. Every Friday night mum and aunt Lillian would attend Mrs Rodwell's sewing classes in Hawley Square, Margate. My mum made all of my clothes. She was particularly good at creating the most beautiful ball gowns decorated with thousands of tiny glass beads all carefully sewn on by her delicate fingers. Her pride and joy was making my wedding dress back in 1978.

It was while I was browsing in Madam Popoff Vintage that the idea for my novel was conceived. Friends have told me that this is a woman's book and they are probably right. It is a work of fiction based on a vintage clothing store. However, I do want to be very clear, the Madam Popoff of my novel; her shop, its staff, customers and the stories that I have written bear no resemblance to the real Madam Popoff or to any other person except for the story of the lovely tablecloths. My father did sew those when he was recovering from pulmonary TB. They are one of my most treasured possessions. Essentially my book is a work of fiction. I do encourage readers to visit the real shop and to meet the lovely owner, Deborah. Her own life story and more information about her vintage fashion shop can be found on www.madampopoff.com

For many years I have worked in the field of holistic healing. I really love what I do and I've had the great privilege of working with so many wonderful clients and colleagues. However, I have always wanted to reach a wider audience in my work. *"Last Train to Margate"* is a book that embraces healing. The fictitious Madam Popoff shares pearls of wisdom and when her student, Poppy, discovers a little booklet called *"The Twelve Healers,"* by Dr. Edward Bach Poppy's life is forever changed. Poppy begins to see with an inner vision, she begins to truly acknowledge the intricacies of life, the key that emotions play in our wellbeing and how letting go, forgiveness, compassion, gratitude and love steer us towards calmer waters and to a better sense of wellbeing.

I have many people to thank but most important of all I want to dedicate my book to the very fond memory of my very loving mum and dad, Evelyn and Pat Forrester, to my dear uncle, Len Hewson, and to the brave lifeboat men of *The Lord Southborough* and the Margate Surf Boat, *Friend To All Nations.*

Over the years my life has been blessed with many wisdom teachers but I would like to offer special thanks to my aunt, Lillian Hewson, and to Misha Norland, Jeremy Sherr, Dr. Jacob Mirman, Sujata Owens, Cilla Whatcott, Hanna and Gisela Kroeger, Jeanette Rohrpasser, Sister Rosalind Gefre and Kevin Doheny.

They say that when the student is ready the teacher appears. I always recall the day, many years ago, when I was browsing in a Minnesota bookstore when suddenly a book fell off the shelf and landed on my foot. It was a book about Bach flower remedies. I have always loved gardening and painting flowers. On that day I made an impulsive purchase. This book changed my life. Dr. Edward Bach has become one of my greatest wisdom teachers. I have a lot to thank him for and I feel his presence in my life daily. He has helped to bring grace and balance to my life and I look to his writings for guidance in all of my work. In 2006 I completed my studies as a Registered Bach Practitioner. *(Sally Lynn Tamplin.)* In many ways *"Last Train to Margate"* is my attempt to bring the wisdom of Edward Bach to an even wider audience. I do hope that in some small way my book may be life changing for my readers too. If you would like to discover more about the life and work of Edward Bach please take a look at the Bach Centre web site www.bachcentre.com

Friends have asked me if I have some favourite stories from my book. The story of the little gold donkey brooch seemed to write itself. I love animals, when I was younger I was very keen on horses and spent much of my spare time either riding or hanging out at The George Hill Stables near my home. My uncle Len told me how his father, Cecil Hewson, had been in the trenches in World War 1. One night he was in no man's land with fellow engineers and they got lost. One of the men knew how to read the night sky and it was the stars that led them back to safety. Just recently my husband and I were sailing our yacht 50 miles from land off the coast of Key West, Florida. There was no light pollution being so far from land, the night sky was brilliant and it made me really appreciate the majesty of the stars.

I also love the story of the exquisite iris clutch bag and its connection to the lifeboat family. I had my first sailing boat when I was 12 years old, a Mirror Dinghy. I really enjoyed sailing it in Margate harbour and by the pier. Mum, dad and I were members of Margate Yacht Club for many years and we've all had connections with the lifeboats and fundraising. The RNLI has always been close to our hearts. If you take the time to read more about the life of Dr. Edward Bach you will discover that he had a very special connection to the lifeboat men of Cromer in Norfolk. My uncle Len shared his memories with me of the evacuation of Dunkirk. He was a young lad at the time and he recalled going with his father, Cecil, to the Arcadian Hotel and helping out as the soldiers were brought ashore by the little ships and *The Lord Southborough*. Uncle Len and his father knew Ted and the Parker family.

Acknowledgements

I am most grateful to and want to particularly thank and acknowledge my editor, Frank Skinner. Frank is the father of Elizabeth, my good friend since childhood. He has known me since I was seven years old. Frank was head of the English Department at Hartsdown Secondary School, Margate and has currently enjoyed many years of active retirement.

My dear friend, Marilyn Pafford, and my aunt, Lillian Hewson, have spent hours hearing me read my initial manuscripts. They encouraged me to complete my book and to begin its sequel *"Ramsgate Calling."* Thank you both for your time, love, encouragement and support!

Although this is a work of fiction there are facts and details pertaining to Margate, its history and people. I have used local sources, a few books and web sites to help provide me with background information and they are listed below. I have tried to check things carefully but if the reader finds any errors please forgive me!

Margate Lifeboat Station, The Rendezvous, Margate, Kent, CT9 1HG

Spitfire and Hurricane Memorial Museum, The Airfield, Manston Road, Ramsgate Kent, CT12 5DF

Margate Museum, Market Place, Margate, CT9 1EN

www.historyof.place - The Royal School for Deaf Children, Margate

www.theatreroyalmargate.com

www.albanytaxicharity.org

www.kentww1.com

www.homeopathyworks.com
"Calendula - one of homeopathy's many gifts to humankind."
Posted by Dr. Lisa Samet N.D. on Jan 12th 2018

"Wikipedia.org" for checking facts especially relating to the evacuation of Dunkirk, battles of World War 1, Sarah Thorne and The Theatre Royal, Margate and the history of The Venice Carnival.

"The History of the Royal Sea Bathing Hospital, Margate, 1791 – 1991" F.G. Strange

"Margate: A photographic history of your town (Francis Frith collection.)" Alan Kay

"Around Thanet. Photographic Memories (Francis Frith Collection.)" Helen Livingston

"Ramsgate and Thanet Life. In Old Photographs." D.R.J. Perkins

"The Medical Discoveries of Edward Bach Physician." Nora Weeks

"The Twelve Healers." Edward Bach

www.bachcentre.com

Lightning Source UK Ltd.
Milton Keynes UK
UKHW020630170719
346313UK00005B/99/P